SPECIAL MESSAGE TO READERS

THE ULVERSCROFT FOUNDATION
(registered UK charity number 264873)

wa
resea   s.

- T   lye
  l
- T   eat
  (
- l   nd
  t   gy,
  l
- T   ip,
  l
- T   rn
  (
- T   yal

You   on
l
Eve   u
wc
re

THE ULVERSCROFT FOUNDATION
The Green, Bradgate Road, Anstey
Leicester LE7 7FU, England
Tel: (0116) 236 4325

website: www.foundation.ulverscroft.com

Martin Bannister was born in Wigan, Lancashire. He studied fine art and has worked as a freelance artist, graffiti muralist, teacher and support worker for people with enduring mental health problems. A graduate of the Creative Writing MA at the University of East Anglia, he lives and works in London.

A MAP OF NOWHERE

David Price always wished life would blow up in his face. And then it did. His mother died; the urge to paint left him; and Sarah came his way — followed by Pete, a psychiatric outpatient. Now David spends his time worrying about Sarah's eating habits, visiting her terminally ill sister, and working as Pete's carer. When Pete's odd behaviour starts to leave David fearing for his own safety, he is shocked to discover that Sarah knows the reason why — but will not disclose it . . .

MARTIN BANNISTER

A MAP OF NOWHERE

Complete and Unabridged

ULVERSCROFT
Leicester

First published in Great Britain in 2013 by
Legend Press Ltd
London

First Large Print Edition
published 2015
by arrangement with
Legend Press Ltd
London

A catalogue record for this book is available
from the British Library.

ISBN 978–1–4448–2576–3

Published by
F. A. Thorpe (Publishing)
Anstey, Leicestershire

Set by Words & Graphics Ltd.
Anstey, Leicestershire
Printed and bound in Great Britain by
T. J. International Ltd., Padstow, Cornwall

This book is printed on acid-free paper

For Max, my boys and my dad.

Acknowledgements

Firstly I'd like to thank three women who helped set me on the path to writing this book: Alison Fell who persuaded me to try something longer than a short story, Michèle Roberts who read it in its early stages, and the late Pat Kavanagh whose letter saying she'd like to represent me I kept, framed and still look at from time to time.

Also huge thanks to all those who have looked at the book in its various drafts over the years — Kezia Martin, Mary Crisp, Ricky, Rose, Alison, Seth Fishman, Clare Lusher. Thanks to Mark Gravil for being my cool-headed, go-to technical advisor, Julian Hanshaw for getting the cover design just right, Mark Alesky for the great photographs, and Miranda Sawyer for pointing out that tragic can also be funny.

Thanks to my inspiring and determined agent, Sophie Lambert, who told me we'd get there in the end.

To Lauren Parsons, Tom Chalmers and Lucy Boguslawski at Legend Press.

To my dad who told me never to give up trying.

To Dieter who agreed.

And finally to Max who, having heard that someone had said yes, bunked off work so that we could jump into a taxi and celebrate.

What becomes of all the little boys
who run away from home,
the world just keeps on getting bigger
once you get out on your own.
Tom Waits

The important thing
is the obvious thing
nobody is saying.
William S. Burroughs

I

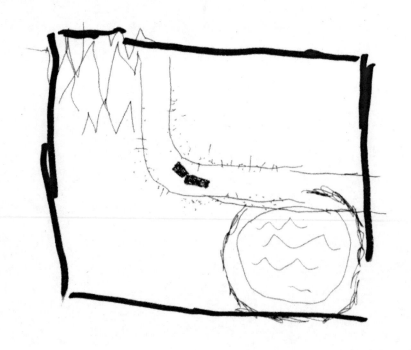

Peter Doran
<u>A Map of Nowhere</u>
Marker pen and pencil on paper

1

The team are concerned about him again. There have been warning signs.

Last week, according to a bank statement I found, he withdrew his last £122 and closed down his account. Two days after that he called his adopted sister, who he hasn't spoken to in fifteen years, to apologise for 'everything that happened when they were children'. Then on Wednesday, completely out of the blue, he matter-of-factly informed me that it was a myth that injecting air into a vein would kill you, and that what usually happens when someone takes a bath with a toaster is that the fuse simply blows. Equally as worrying are the notes from last week's psychiatric assessment. Paragraph three circled in red pen. Certain words and phrases high-lighted in yellow: Peter appears less anxious; Peter seems well-balanced.

This isn't quite as positive as it might sound. Clients often appear like this shortly before ending it all. Suddenly at peace with the world, no longer in turmoil, they know where they're going and feel in control of when they'll get there. Which is comforting for them. And unusual. For once *they* get to say when things happen. *They* draw the timeline.

Five three-hour visits a week are what I make here. I'm his part-time key worker. We cook. We watch TV. Now and again we take a short walk. That, in total, is only fifteen relatively safe hours out of the one hundred and sixty eight that make up Monday to Sunday. A small percentage. All that time on his hands. All those unattended moments in which he could take pills, gas or hang himself, open up veins in the bath, stick wet fingers in a light socket, or go to bed with a plastic bag over his head, an elastic band securing it around his throat. And then, of course, there's the great outdoors to go at. Bridges and cliffs to leap from. Cars, trains, buses to step in front of. Lakes, rivers, the sea to drown in. He could even make a public menace of himself, wave a toy gun at the police, go out with a bang and a front-page obituary.

Something tells me, though, that if he succeeds this time, the act itself will be more creative, some method outside my thinking. Whatever he does dream up, I just hope I'm not the one who finds him. I like him, I do, but I don't need that at the moment; judging by the letter I received two days ago it seems he's already got me into enough trouble as it is.

It was anonymous and brief. Black pen on beige paper: *I now know who you are and where you live.*

I have a pretty good idea who sent it and should probably call the police. But that would only make things worse. That's how the whole thing started in the first place.

The incident report describes how last month, or more specifically . . . *on April 2nd at 9.53 a.m., at the junction of Herne Hill road/Croxted road* . . . Pete and I were heading over the zebra crossing, intending to head into Brockwell park.

We didn't get there. Because for no good reason, Pete suddenly decided to lie face down in the road (this was the start of his decline and things have been getting steadily worse day by day). Smiling to himself, eyes closed and moaning with pleasure, he nuzzled his cheek against the tarmac as though it were a freshly washed pillowcase. Traffic was already backing up as far as I could see — the road is busy at that time in the morning because of a nearby primary school — and at the front of the queue was a man in a silver van.

I waved an apology to him — he was around my age with spiky blond hair and a skull-like face — but he was clearly not in the mood to be held up. A young black woman who was passing by crossed over to ask if everything was okay, and she got down on her knees to talk to Pete. 'Look at the weather, darling,' she said to him. 'Wouldn't you rather be in the park than lying in the middle of a dirty road?' At this point silver van man honked his horn and raised his hands, but the woman pulled a face and raised hers in return, mocking him for his impatience. He didn't like this, didn't like it at all, and he leaned out of the window and shouted that we should *get a fucking move on*. Pete immediately got to his feet and obligingly walked to the kerb. Silver van man slipped into gear, and as he pulled away he threw something at the woman, which hit her on the back.

As it turned out, it was only balled up chips in greasy paper, the remains of the man's lunch from who knows when. The woman simply laughed the whole thing off and said she felt sorry for men like that.

I couldn't let it go though. It stayed with me all day. And that evening I reported what had happened to the police.

They said I'd done the right thing. Yes, it was only chips, but it could just as easily have been something else. Two weeks later they called to say they'd traced the van and questioned the driver, who claimed to have done no such thing. Nevertheless he'd been charged and would be appearing before a magistrate.

By then I'd begun to see how ridiculous the whole thing seemed. I pictured people in court, particularly the jury, sniggering and shaking their heads as I gave evidence from behind a screen. Not that it would make much difference. Silver van man had already been given my name. Apparently it's normal procedure for it to appear on the witness statement. Not the address or any other details, just the name.

No words of comfort or support are to be found at home. According to Sarah, I have only myself to blame. Last night, in the middle of what she was keen to point out was a disagreement and not an argument, she said that silver van man probably traced my whereabouts through a social networking site.

'It makes no difference that you don't do Facebook,' she shrugged. 'Friends of friends of friends could have put stuff up on there about you. It happens to me all the time. I regularly see photos of myself that I can't even remember having posed for. My advice? Don't go fighting battles for people who haven't asked you to and you'll find life a lot simpler, trust me.'

We went back to watching a documentary about Vermeer — who, it turns out, painted all those tranquil interiors — *Woman Reading a Letter at a Window*, *Girl with Pearl Earring* etc — because his own home life was so chaotic. 'Yes,' I joked. 'I know *that* feeling.' Which Sarah seemed to find wildly amusing. 'Chaos?' she said. 'You? You don't know the meaning of the word. You've lived too safe a life, paddling in the shallow end of your own but diving straight in the deep end of everyone else's. Try focusing on what's closer to home for once. Try that and see what happens.'

$\star$ $\star$ $\star$

I lean back against the cooker and yawn loudly into my hand. Pete shuffles by, his arms loaded up with damp washing.

'Sorry,' I say. 'Slept badly.'

'You'll be free to go soon.'

I hold up my cup. 'Refill?'

'Why not.'

I flick the kettle on and open the door of the wall cupboard. It's a sad affair. Bottom shelf: two rows of white Ikea mugs and a box of Typhoo. Middle: a tin of custard powder and some loose black peppercorns. Top:

8

empty, unused. Pete isn't a tall man.

I amble over to the back door and watch him peg his pink shirts out on the line. 'We should start cooking soon.'

He stoops to pick up a sock. 'Two minutes.'

'I'll make a start with the onion.'

'What are you making?'

'We are making shepherd's pie.'

He sniggers.

The two of us have an odd, imbalanced relationship. I know a lot about him. He knows next to nothing about me. He doesn't know, for example, that I once worked as a carpenter, or that I used to smoke — though nothing to match his terrifying intake. He's never seen any of my paintings, doesn't know that one of them won a national competition and hung for a while in the Royal Academy. He isn't aware that I've been hospitalised only twice in my life — the first time in this country, the second time in India. He doesn't know that Sarah's thirty-one year old sister Clare is dying of cancer in a hospice in Hampstead, or that my mother died four months ago of the same illness. None of this will ever come up in conversation over tea and biscuits. My life will remain a mystery to him. Professional boundaries say that's the way it has to be.

Most of what I know about him I've read

rather than heard. There are his case notes — two sides of A4, a list of key events that have contributed to the decline in his mental health. And then there's the suicide handout, a far more interesting self-penned account of his last psychotic episode.

Pete was born with a rare disorder called exstrophy — a severe deformity of the genitals, so severe that some male cases are sexually re-assigned at birth. He wasn't; he was put up for adoption instead. The couple who took him on already had a daughter but couldn't seem to get pregnant again. He was two when he moved in with them, and he's described those early years as the only happy ones he ever had. Just before his ninth birthday his mother was killed in a car crash. He saw it all. The whole family was in the car.

That's enough for anyone. But it gets worse.

He grew up (sort of) and when he was sixteen his father died of a heart attack. Alone in the world suddenly — his sister had by this time moved abroad — he met a woman called Pat and quickly married her, despite his sexual inadequacies. He soon discovered that Pat had her own problems, one of them alcoholism. Six weeks into their shambles of a marriage he caught her in bed with someone else. Not long after that she threw herself from the balcony of their eighth story flat in Bermondsey. Pete was sectioned two days later and spent his longest spell to date in psychiatric care.

Which is how he met his second wife, Iris.

Now, I'm all for the story of how you meet someone being an interesting one. The story can be your base coat, your primer — it's what the whole picture can hang on. There are limits, though, surely (I mean, longevity does seem pretty unlikely for a couple who've both recently attempted suicide).

Surprisingly, Pete and Iris' marriage lasted for nine years but broke down a year ago when Iris met another man, John, her present husband.

Over the last six months Pete's been an outpatient at the Maudesley hospital in Camberwell. He's recently had a course of Electroconvulsive Therapy, and although it seems to have worked to some degree, he claims it's erased certain events from his memory, left him hearing occasional whispering voices — one male, one female — and gifted him with psychic powers.

★ ★ ★

Tea made, I help him hang out the rest of the washing. He uses only the yellow pegs so I

11

introduce a few blues and purples to make things interesting. 'Colour can resurrect a dead day,' I tell him.

'Not this one.'

Back in the kitchen, ten minutes later, I suggest the medium-sized frying pan.

After wiping it out with kitchen roll, Pete sets it gently on the hob.

'Olive oil,' I suggest.

He shakes his head. 'I saw on TV that you shouldn't use it for cooking. It gives you cancer if you heat it up.' He heads over to the fridge. 'Keep an eye on the pan. It's new.' He takes out the mince and closes the fridge door. But then he just stands there, the tray hanging from his hand, eyes in a sidelong glance, head cocked as if listening to someone whispering in his ear.

This kind of thing. Invisible presences. Muttered conversations with ghosts. Post-it notes on the fridge to friends and family members long since dead. This is what I find interesting about him (not to mention the eerie connection between our mothers, which I still haven't told him about, and probably never will). He isn't mad (when on medication), not in the traditional sense of the word. He never cut off one of his own hands in a public library or ran around the streets half-naked, ranting and eating food from bins. He never straddled a police officer and stabbed him repeatedly with a kitchen knife through his bulletproof vest. He doesn't hang his wet washing on live cables he's torn from the ceiling or collect cigarette butts and rotting fruit in catering size coffee tins. His 'indications' are subtle. You have to be on the lookout for them.

Don't get me wrong, he's had his moments, and he'd be the first to admit it. Now and again, when we're pottering about like this — cooking, opening post, just chatting — he'll ask if I've taken a look at the suicide handout recently. 'You should,' he'll tell me. 'You know, just to remind yourself how bad things can get. So you're aware of what you're dealing with.'

We recently had a conversation about our names. Mine is David Price. His is Peter Doran.

'Our initials would be the same if one of us reversed them,' he said excitedly.

When I told him my middle name was Andrew (his is Philip) he was devastated.

His new thing seems to be apples. There's a definite apple thing going on at the moment. I'll find an apple in a place where an apple shouldn't be — in the bedroom, in the bath, on top of the DVD player, trophy like. And every now and again lately he'll give me this

13

look, a searching look that suggests he's trying to read my mood before breaking something to me, something I might find difficult.

★ ★ ★

Another five minutes have limped by. The onion has browned nicely and we've added rosemary and oregano. Ginger got the thumbs down because it won't go with what we're making. It's fine with spices but not herbs. He's learned a lot about seasoning since we met.

'Now the mince.'

Lips pursed, he stabs at the cling-film. Meaty air puffs out through the hole. 'Its last breath,' he laughs.

'How are you doing for money?'

'So so.'

'Enough for the weekend?'

'Should be okay.' He stares contemplatively at the pan's contents. 'How will I know when this is done?'

'By checking for pinkness underneath. Give me the spoon. Open a tin of tomatoes and get a pan for the potatoes.'

'Do we need a colander?'

'No, it will just make more washing up.'

'I like washing up. When I'm washing up I forget everything.'

I am not here to save him. It's important to

remind myself of this. Care work is mostly maintenance and distraction, not Super-heroics. My remit is to listen, give support, cook, encourage him to eat, and keep things upbeat whenever possible.

I do some tidying up. I can also stretch to this. As I'm vacuuming, Pete decides that now is as good a time as any to clip his fingernails. He sits down at the kitchen table and takes the gold hairdressing scissors from the drawer. I wipe down the work surface and wait patiently as he snips and files. Time will drag now the preparation phase is over. Just waiting. Clock watching. It's still only 10.15.

I go and put out the rubbish. As I pass the bedroom window I notice that the curtains are still closed. This is also a fairly recent thing. Not a good sign. Pete joins me in the garden after a while, and for the next five or so minutes I watch him wander around the borders, stooping occasionally to look at flowers and weeds. He stops in front of the apple tree, places his palms against the trunk, and closes his eyes as if channeling some mysterious energy. Suddenly snapping out of his trance, he turns my way. 'I wonder how *you* would have coped with the life I've had.' He points a shaking finger at me. 'Big things could be coming your way. You just never know. Be ready.'

'Good big things?'

'Matter of opinion.'

'I'll hope for the best.'

Ten minutes later the potatoes are still a little hard, but it's too late, we've run out of time. We hurry through the final stages. I add a spoonful of butter, salt and pepper. Then I mash. Pete tips the mince and onion into the square earthenware dish. I spoon on the potato, flatten it down and then make ridges in it with a fork.

'Why are you doing that?'

'Decoration. The ridges brown and crisp in the oven. They're the best bit. Leave it in for about twenty-five to thirty minutes. Not much longer or it will burn. More importantly, don't forget to get some of it inside you before you go drinking.'

2

It's Sunday lunchtime and I'm at the studio — a classroom in what used to be a primary school in the run-down part of Greenwich. I've spent most of the morning tidying up. I've swept up coils of peeled-off masking tape, binned dried-up decorators brushes, offcuts of canvas and screwed up sketches. It gets like this every couple of months and a fresh start can make a big difference.

I pick up and re-read the note I found taped to my door when I got in. *A man came to see you yesterday but he said he'd come back another time. Kate from studio 14.* My first thought (and hope) was that it was someone art related, a gallery owner perhaps, or agent. Much more likely, though, is my new pen friend — silver van man.

I hang up one of last week's paintings and stand back to look at it. It's of a pair of blue thighs seen as though you, the viewer, are peering down at them. It's supposed to evoke the strange feeling of seeing your legs in a new pair of jeans, the momentary shock of the unfamiliar.

My paintings were once described by an art

17

critic as treading the line between moving and comical, which I think is a fair compliment. It's difficult enough to achieve either of those. To get both in one hit is something else.

The blue needs to be darker, so I mix up a new batch, which I'm just about to start applying when there's a timid knock on the door.

It turns out to be Kate.

Kate's paintings are all dark stormy landscapes. There's an underlying sadness to everything about her — her shaky voice, her Cleopatra-style black bob, her ruddy complexion. I like her but try not to spend too much time in her company. She's clearly lonely, intrusive as a direct result, and her melancholy can influence my colour choices.

'Hi,' she says gloomily. 'Did you get the note about your friend?'

'Yes, thanks.'

'He didn't seem like the type of person you'd hang out with.'

'No? Why's that? What did he look like?'

To my relief she describes my visitor as fairly small with dark hair.

'Not much to go on.'

'I'm not very good at remembering people. I'd be rubbish in one of those line-ups.'

'Was his hair parted at the side, a bit like Hitler's?'

'Maybe. I think so.'

18

'And did he say what he wanted?'

She shakes her head. 'No, he just said he needed to find you but it could wait.'

I look down at the brush in my hand, then give the paint a stir with it.

'Okay,' she says. 'I'd best leave you to it.'

'Thanks for passing on the message. Have a good afternoon.'

I close the door and continue stirring the paint, relieved that my visitor wasn't who I thought it was but baffled as to why Pete would head over here on a Sunday. How does he even know where it is? I call him (he has a mobile but rarely answers it). Predictably it goes straight to voicemail. I leave a message to call back, which he almost certainly won't do.

I return to the painting and add the blue. It makes a world of difference. The blue thighs are now two dark towers set against the bright yellow background — a rug. The rug should be striped. Suddenly that seems obvious. The tassles may also need some work; they're much too uniform and not at all tassle-like. I mix up three new colours — khaki, lemon yellow, dark grey — glancing over at the art postcards stapled to my tool cupboard door. A few Van Goghs' — *Bedroom at Arles, Trees in Winter* — Hopper's *Morning on Cape Cod*, and a black and brown Tàpies that looks like the underside of a shabby old sofa. There's also a postcard of one of my own paintings — *Happy Accident* — in which a blind accordion player is emerging from a dark forest leaving behind an avenue of accidentally felled trees.

★ ★ ★

I always wanted to be an artist. At school I'd deliberately get sent out of maths so that I could head to the art room (the maths teacher was glad to see the back of me, and the art teacher didn't mind me being there as long as I was working). For my exam I turned in three views of the same valley seen through trees — one in greens, one in blues, one in reds. A castle occupied the green valley, a futuristic glass domed city the blue, and in the red valley all that remained was a burnt out post-apocalyptic wasteland. At leavers open evening, the head teacher took my mother to one side and asked if there was a history of depression in the family.

I remember the feeling of sheer panic as I walked away from school towards her waiting car on the last day. I had absolutely no idea what I'd be doing next, and that was pretty strange. I also vividly remember hanging my uniform up and staring at it for a long time, thinking how odd it was that I'd never have to wear it again.

A week later I'd started a carpentry apprenticeship.

We made hand built kitchens. I spent a month sanding down doors and drawer fronts until the tips of my fingers bled and my fingerprints virtually disappeared. Then I was promoted to using a mortising machine. Then a circular saw. On Mondays I'd go with the boss to measure up a new job. The rest of the week we'd spend machining up the wood, assembling the units, they'd be spray painted or varnished at the weekend, and fitted the following week. It was interesting work in some ways. I got to meet people, learned a craft, found out what wood could do. By the age of twenty, though, I was tired of coming home with my hair and eyes full of sawdust.

So I travelled for a while — Europe mainly, went to France and Greece and ended up spending a year in Germany because I met a girl. Doro was half Indian/half German and had a tattoo of a wolf on her shoulder. That was a big part of what attracted me to her. She was also fiercely intelligent. I thought about moving over there permanently, worked a series of terrible jobs to get a more realistic idea about how that would feel — building site work, delivery driving, I even worked in a chicken processing factory. That was the worst job I've ever had. All I had to do, morning after morning, was make a particular incision on the breast of the hanging birds as they endlessly swung by me. The smell of chicken offal never quite leaves your skin if you're exposed to it day in, day out.

And I'd thought sawdust was bad.

In the end I missed England, and I returned wondering what to do with myself. I decided to apply to do an Art foundation course and was offered a place.

My parents weren't unsupportive, just too wrapped up in their own lives to take too much notice of where mine was heading. I moved back in with them and soon discovered that things were worse than I remembered. They'd bickered all my life, but now that I was a little older, with a few experiences under my belt, I began to see their marriage in a way I never had before. Apart from the usual suspects — money, lack of communication — both of which I'd always heard references to, I suddenly got the feeling that there was some other problem, something big and fundamentally wrong.

I wasn't likely to find out what it was. If I ever asked, they denied everything, claimed that all families had stuff going on. Concealment played a large part whenever they went head to head. Cryptic phrases and coded language featured heavily. My dad's favourite was, 'Oh, we're back onto *you know what* again, are we?' My mother seemed to favour, 'The past is the past, Alan. It's too late now. Maybe you should have thought about that at the time.'

That year turned out (for me, at least) to be a good one — mainly because I spent most of it immersed in art. I travelled down to London and visited every major gallery. I went to Amsterdam, revisited Berlin, and met some friends who I still speak to from time to time. Mainly, though, I worked hard to get together a strong portfolio of work. I sent it off to Birmingham University and it got me a foot in the door.

I still like my Foundation portfolio. It has a naïve honesty about it that can easily get lost once you start a degree course. Then, every idea has to be backed up and justified. You have to know your onions and be able to talk about them in an historical context.

Knowledge isn't always power. Too much of it can bog you down.

My graduation show, three years later, was a success. I made a series of large-scale paintings of fingers plucking blades of grass and being sliced open in the process. The fingertips were huge on the canvas, filling it almost, the fingerprint whorls — sometimes dark grey, sometimes a yellowy white

— acting as decoration and looking like contour lines on an Ordinance Survey map. The wounds looked genuinely painful. I got a first and sold every painting.

It seemed the logical thing to do to head further south, so I came to London. With the money I'd made from the show I rented a cheap studio, found somewhere to live, and signed on. My work improved over the next few years and I began to make a name for myself.

But the bubble was about to burst.

I decided to go to India for a few months. I'd heard that anyone with an interest in colour should see it. I got sick in Calcutta. At first they thought I had cerebral malaria but it turned out to be amoebic dysentry. I ended up in the Belle Vue Hospital for two weeks, and when I got out I came straight home.

I went to visit my parents shortly after returning. I stayed for a day or two and then headed back to London. A few days later I got a call from my mother. She'd had a stomach upset and hoped I hadn't passed anything 'exotic' on to her. The upset didn't get any better, and after two weeks she went to see the doctor. Three days later she was diagnosed with bowel cancer.

There are cancer survivors. I know one personally. The man in the studio below only has one lung and cycles in here everyday.

Somehow, though, I knew from the start that my mother wouldn't be one of the lucky ones. She didn't want to fight the illness. Within six months I barely recognised her.

One thing Sarah has told me about cancer is that it finds buried anger and latches on to it. That's what she believes. I don't know if I agree, but who knows — my mother had definitely been angry about something for as long as I could remember.

I did a painting of her just before she died, but my gallery didn't like it, and it was at this point that they decided to let me go. My work, they claimed, was moving in a direction they felt they couldn't market.

In my opinion the painting is one of my best. It captures my mother's spirit perfectly.

It's called: *Sick Woman Flicks Spinach Across a Room From a Wooden Spoon.*

A good title should speak for itself.

*　*　*

It's just gone 7 p.m. and I'm back home. I close the front door behind me and can see Sarah in the kitchen. She's half-dressed and preparing food, though probably not for herself.

Eating isn't something she seems to do much of lately, and she's lost a considerable amount of weight over the last few months.

She's half the curvy woman I met back in November. Her shoulder blades are terrifyingly prominent; they remind me of the tip of a pair of scissors being pushed against a leather belt to form a new hole. A fine downy hair has started to grow on her stomach and hips as though nature has decided to step in to protect her from the cold. She puts the weight loss down to the stress of Clare's illness, but I've suspected from the start that she and food have a bit of a history.

'Hi,' she says as I come into the kitchen. 'How did it go?'

'Okay. Are you going out somewhere?'

'Yes.'

'You didn't say anything earlier.'

'I didn't know earlier.'

'Anywhere nice?'

'The hospice. Clare asked if I'd stay over tonight.'

'Oh, I see.'

She walks past me into the bedroom and I follow her in there. 'Pete went to my studio yesterday.'

She clatters clothes up and down the rail. 'Really?'

'Did you tell him where it was?'

'No. Of course not.'

Sarah is the reason I know Pete. She was the one who got me the job as his key worker.

She's worked on and off in mental health for years but gave it up recently to spend more time with Clare.

'I think the letter was probably from him too.'

'Why do you say that?'

'Just a feeling. What do you think he could have wanted?'

She holds two pairs of trousers out in front of her — jeans and brown cords. After some thoughtful study she goes for the cords. 'I've no idea. Ask him when you see him on Monday. How is he lately, anyway?'

'He seems preoccupied. I think he's keeping something from me.'

'Like what?'

'I've no idea.'

'You think everyone's keeping something from you, David.' She turns her back to me. 'You do it with me all the time.' She takes off her vest, wraps her black bra around her waist and swivels it into position. 'If there is something, I'm sure it will come out sooner or later.' She begins brushing her hair, her head hanging forwards. 'I miss not seeing him. It's good that he has you, and that the two of you get on.'

'We don't always. Sometimes I think he'd rather I wasn't there at all.'

'I doubt that's true.' She pulls a tangle from

the hairbrush and gathers her hair together. As she's looping the hair tie in place, the pebble-like bumps of her spine roll around under her skin.

'I can see your ribs.'

'Don't.'

'I'm just saying.'

'Well please don't.' Close to the mirror now, her nose only inches from it, she draws on some eyeliner and gently bats at her lashes with her finger. She slips the half pencil into her back pocket and turns to face me. 'I'd better go. I told Clare I'd be there by eight.'

'Have you already eaten?' I ask pointlessly.

'I don't have time.'

'I could make a bagel. You could take it with you.'

'No. Thanks though. Are you still okay to come to the hospice tomorrow?'

'Yes, I'll come when I'm done at Pete's.'

'Okay. I'll call if I need you to collect anything on the way.' Her eyes go to a cup on the floor by the bed. 'If you wash up, please can you remember to rinse, especially the cups, and not when they're upside down on the drainer. The insides stay soapy that way.'

'Got it. Insides and out.'

'Good. Oh, and don't forget to close the microwave door. You left it open yesterday.'

3

Mental illness is fascinating and terrifying in equal measure, and Open Door has seen pretty much everything. People who hoard junk mail, scraps of carpet, engine parts, ancient electrical appliances with the cords cut off. People who write down the registration number of every car that passes by their living room window. People who have their hair cut every day. People who haven't had a haircut in twenty years. People with black teeth. People with black fingernails. People with black toilets. Obsessive compulsives hooked into the living hell of constant lock checking.

One client — a not unattractive woman — was at one time a fairly well-known illustrator/animator — never out of work, no predisposition towards mental illness. But then an intense, high profile ad campaign for a big brand soft drink led to a repetitive strain injury on her wrist. No longer able to work, she became depressed. A suicide attempt followed. Medication. Deeper depression. For two years. Persistent insomnia resulted in her taking late night walks. Until she was hit by a car. She survived, with serious head injuries, and her life now consists of smoking, drinking coffee, and reading newspapers down at the Lady Gomm Day Centre.

This is the terrifying half of the equation. Terrifying because clearly anyone from any walk of life can so easily slip off the edge of it. If, like me, you always suspected things could go awry, then the fear is even more prevalent. When my mother was in the final stages of her cancer, my mind felt so overloaded, so cluttered, I suspected I was heading for some sort of breakdown myself. I once found myself stopped on a street corner, a street corner I must have stood on or walked around a thousand times. But there I was, and I recognised absolutely nothing. Then panic set in. Which made things worse. In the end I had to ask someone where I was. I've never experienced confusion like that.

Pete's suicide handout is the fascinating half. Crammed full of crazy detail and description of what mental illness feels like, it's the kind of stuff creative people secretly dream of experiencing, providing they can a) survive and b) recover sufficiently afterwards in order to paint, write or sing about it. He prepared it because he'd grown weary of repeating the story of his life, in particular those final weeks leading up to what was supposed to be the end of it. His case notes are a dry chronological trudge through history. If anyone wants to actually feel what his life has been like, they should forget the whos, whens and wheres and refer to the handout instead. It's all about the decline itself, he says, not the reasons for it.

He describes psychosis as an excruciating intermittent pain in his head that feels like sandpaper being dragged over his brain. This is his brain at its worst, how it was in those weeks leading up to Christmas day when he planned to throw himself in front of a bus, provided they were running.

He'd stopped taking his medication, and already the signs were there. He could no longer eat his daily fix of chicken soup (his favourite meal) because the bowl would hover off the table every time he tried to get his spoon in. People in the street were whispering about his 'cherub like appearance and long fingernails'. And although he lived alone, he woke up one morning to find a man in a white string vest and yellow shorts sitting in a striped deckchair in his kitchen.

Whoever would read the handout should, he said, imagine having a gifted IQ status of 145 at 5 years old, 120 at 11 years old, and only 95 at 16 years old. There it was, on paper; as the years had gone by he'd quite literally been losing his mind. The volume controls on anger, fear, aggression, bitterness, hatred, and guilt had steadily risen to a level he could no longer tolerate. Like the Steve Miller Band song *Abracadabra*, he'd grown up to be someone who secretly 'heated up but couldn't cool down'.

I have to confess (though I feel bad about it) I laughed out loud when I read this.

Pete had trained as a teacher. But the children hated him (he believed) and refused to take him seriously. Somehow they got wind of his medical condition and one day he walked into the classroom to find *DICK-LESS DORAN* written on the blackboard in huge capitals. His position untenable, he resigned and never taught again. Instead, he resorted to a series of temporary jobs, filing, packing or wrapping goods in cellophane.

During the lead up to Christmas he talks of not actually living seconds and minutes and hours of days at all, at least not in the way he ever had before. Time was different. It did it's own thing, made its own rules. He describes it as like watching a film with someone who keeps pressing different buttons on the DVD remote control. Play. Fast Forward. Pause. Fast Forward. Skip. Play. Irritating and unsettling. One minute he'd be in the bedroom, the next he was on a train, then back in bed, then it was lunchtime and the soup would be hovering again.

Apart from the hovering soup, I know what he means. When I think about how *I* was doing around that time, driving up the motorway, hoping to get there before my mother died, our lives were not too dissimilar, the only difference being I wasn't planning to end mine.

Windows of 'reflective sanity'. And the psychoanalytical term, 'the brief appearance of an observing ego'. He mentions both of these in an incident that happened as he was walking past a pub, where a group of men were huddled in the doorway, smoking. The thought suddenly occurred to him that he might be having some weird ideas. This confused him, because up until now the *way* he was thinking the ideas had seemed perfectly normal. He stopped outside a newsagents to eavesdrop in on what he thought was a scandalous comment at his expense. But this was impossible, by this point the men were at least forty feet away, much too far for clear speech to possibly fall on his ears. This realisation, this first glimpse of what could perhaps be called sane thinking, was something of a relief but at the same time mortifying. In that moment it was clear to him how wrong and untrustworthy his mind had recently become. Not wanting to fully accept this, though, he quickly clouded everything over with another thought: that he was on a path, and whatever happened, he should not deviate from it. This enabled him to turn the episode to his own advantage by convincing himself that what his mind was doing was nothing but a last minute act of sabotage. Never in his life had he seen with such clarity or felt so empowered. Then and there he made the decision to end his life on Christmas Day, the day Jesus had begun his.

Another incident he describes begins with him waking up one morning itching all over. He decided that what he needed was to go to Woolwich Wave Centre for a swim (he'd been before and had always enjoyed himself). This time, though, as soon as he arrived he felt that something was different. As he was standing at the counter, paying his admission, he found he couldn't maintain eye contact with the girl serving. Then he couldn't find his wallet. Then he did find it but didn't have change for the lockers. These things may not sound like much, but they are when you are in the grip of paranoia. A paranoid person can end up throwing himself off a bridge because of something so seemingly trivial (or, indeed, in front of a bus).

When the girl finally handed him his ticket he dropped it, and then when he bent over to pick it up, the contents of his bag — towel, shorts, shampoo, goggles, pretty much everything — spilled out onto the floor. Added to this, he could hear that he'd obviously picked a bad time to come. There was a party of schoolchildren in and he could hear their screams and yells punctuated by shrill bursts of the lifeguard's whistle. Then the voice of a teacher. Stop! Stop! *No!* Then, without knowing how, he was changed and pool-side and the children were splashing about in two closed off lanes, and as he watched them he perceived their screams not to be screams of fun but of fear and distress. He saw the wet surface around the edge of the pool as treacherous, the wave machine as a potential killer, the slide a hazard that could easily result in a small boy or girl breaking his or her neck. He could almost hear the wooden door of the sauna swelling, then jamming from the heat, trapping someone inside to die of dehydration. He got out of there without going anywhere near the water or any of the other death traps.

From that day on, fear and anxiety played an increasingly large part in every moment. Some days he wouldn't leave the house at all. Then he started to stay out all the time. Sometimes, despite the fact that it was December, he'd sleep in the park peace garden. He took up running in order to stop smoking. Then he took up smoking again in order to stop running. Then came a new phase. He started going to church. He went every day. Always the same church and always the same pew. Even if there was nothing special on, he'd go and sit in silence for hours at a time.

This was when he made the decision to allow Him into his life (Him, I'm assuming, meaning God).

At this point (around halfway through) the handout starts to make less sense. Which I suppose makes it a pretty well-paced representation of the decline in his mental state. He suddenly starts to talk of 'seeking Him out', of 'casting a line out into the world and reeling Him in'. He writes that he realises it makes little to no sense to use the 'second' or 'third mind' when it would be far better to use the 'first'. He describes feeling as though he's walking around London during a World War II blackout with a pencil torch, no longer thinking thoughts, his thoughts thinking him. One day, bizarrely, while eating a crusty sandwich, he writes that his jaw came off its hinges. Fortunately he managed to lift it back into position and click it in place. Then one evening, while writing about his day, something mystical happened. As his own narrative became more dramatic, more powerful, more expressive, the sleet on the window pane beat harder, confirming what he'd always known — there was a concrete connection between without and within. There could be no doubt about it. And later, listening to the radio, *Nancy Boy* by Placebo was played. The two references were clearly aimed at him. *Nancy Boy* for his misread homosexuality and Placebo to inform him that the medication he was prescribed two years ago was no longer of any benefit or need to him. Obviously, this meant that death was imminent, and it was now time to listen out for how the suicide act itself should be committed.

It may surprise you to hear that through all of this he was actually holding down a full-time job. He was temping in the offices of a textile firm in East London, and this was where the sign he'd been waiting for presented itself. On December 20th, a man called out to a colleague that, 'he should go by bus.'

Pete stopped what he was doing and walked over to the man's desk. 'I couldn't help overhearing your comment,' he said. 'About the bus.'

The man told him to mind his own business.

'Were you talking about me?'

The man laughed out loud. 'I don't even

know who you are. Are you new? If you must fucking know, I was talking about my brother's car having failed its MOT.'

Clearly this was a cover story. The man had floodlit his exit method for him.

Two days later his supervisor called him in to his office for a chat. There had been reports of run-ins with colleagues. Strange behaviour. Unexplained absences. The chat went on for some time, and the conclusion of it was that they were going to have to let him go. But Pete, by this point, was hardly listening. He was distracted by something. The supervisor's voice had long since faded to nothing, and all of Pete's attention was drawn to his teeth, which were very white and well proportioned. His mouth was moving, and as it did, Pete perceived the teeth to be growing and threatening to fill the room; in that moment he had no doubt whatsoever that this was actually happening. Terrified but at the same time fascinated, he backed away, glancing over his shoulder, checking that his escape route was clear.

Flicking through an A-Z that evening, his eye was drawn to the New King's Road. The plan was now fully in place. He would throw himself under a bus on the New King's Road on Christmas Day. New King's Road was obviously the road of the New King (Jesus) and his suicide would thrust the Old King (Satan) out of him once and for all. This monumental sacrifice would be a far cry from his irrelevant and peripheral existence working in the offices of an East London textile firm.

On Christmas Eve he planned to spend some time in Westminster Cathedral and later visit Covent Garden.

Around lunchtime he took the bus to Victoria station and walked along Victoria Street feeling comforted by all the unfamiliar faces. He arrived at Westminster Cathedral and checked the time. The carol service rehearsal would be halfway through.

Accompanied by the strains of *Silent Night*, and already feeling nauseous from the heavy aroma of Frankincense, he walked slowly and respectfully towards the altar, raising his head now and again to look up at the blackened and impossibly high, arched brick ceiling, which he describes as resembling an infinite starless sky. Then he veered off to the left (pulled by some mysterious force) where before long he found himself passing square pillar after square pillar, each one clad with tall slabs of green, heavily grained marble. Where the slabs met at the corners of the pillars, they mirrored each others grain pattern, creating what looked like towering, moss-coloured vaginas at various degrees of openness. He was repulsed by this, terrified and offended to have such an image forced upon him. But this was a cathedral — God's work was done here.

Relieved, he finally arrived at the mosaic of Jesus' face in the chapel of The Blessed Sacrament. And staring up at it, tears in his eyes, he said a few prayers, one for himself and one for his dead parents. Slowly, in response to the weight of his emotional outpouring, the light green and flesh-tone mosaic tiles of Jesus' face began to shift and swirl, morphing through the full range of human expression — fear, pity, despair, joy, and back to pious empathy. And then out of nowhere a soft deep female voice was whispering in his ear, soothing him and asking how he felt now he'd had time to find out the whole story. Jesus' expression changed again. Now it fixed itself on horror. Pete looked up and cleared his throat. 'I did what you said. I made the journey, the quest. All ends are now tied up. I have seen His image. And I got to see Her light before it went out. You led me there to witness it all, and I'm grateful for that.'

It was around four o'clock by the time he found himself in Covent Garden. Time had jumped on again. Chunks of the day had gone AWOL. He'd cut through St James' Park, that much he knew, but his only real memory of the walk was the ducks and geese and a group of Japanese tourists clogging up the small footbridge he needed to cross.

He'd come to Covent Garden because it was how he wanted to remember London. Roasted sugared almonds and chestnuts. Street entertainers. Carol singers. Christmas, Dickens style.

Detached more than ever from everything and everybody, he wandered around the market observing last minute shoppers. What surprised him was that he felt genuinely happy for them. He could picture them the next morning, sharing the gifts they'd bought. Women trying on earrings. Children eating more gold-wrapped chocolate balls than they should before dinner. Men leaning in to ask wives if aftershave suited them. The only thing that brought the slightest twinge of melancholy was a billboard next to a church celebrating the advent of Faster Broadband. This was the world he was really bidding farewell to. It was important to keep that in mind.

But apart from that, never had December seemed so festive. Mooching around the stalls and shops he began to experience a feeling of deep contentment. At one point a girl with a

French accent wished him *Joyeux Noël*, and without hesitation, and with a benevolent smile on his face, he replied, 'And a very Merry Christmas to you too.'

Because he knew he was saying goodbye to this place, it looked different — real or cinematic. Colours were brighter. Everything seemed to have switched from regular to HD. He sat down on the steps to finish off the stollen and mulled wine he'd bought, and his eyes drank in every detail of what was admittedly a beautiful world. He looked down at his shoes and could picture them weeks or months from now being taken down from a shelf in some charity shop and tried on for size. The thought did not horrify him in the slightest. If anything, he felt a sense of relief that he'd only have to lace them up one more time.

And then, for some reason, he started thinking about Pat, and how the day before she'd jumped from their balcony they'd spent the afternoon together at the Lady Gomm Day Centre, playing cards and dominoes and reading the papers. In the afternoon someone had brought in a stereo and cleared away tables so that anyone who wished to could dance. He could still picture Pat's face clearly. She was the only one dancing, grinning from ear to ear, whooping and twirling around.

He left Covent Garden, and as he made his

way along the Strand he felt a little like he had, at times, when on his way for a haircut — full of doubt (the style suddenly looks better than ever and you wonder if you're doing the right thing by wanting to change it). This was when he realised he wasn't quite as certain as he'd thought about ending his life tomorrow. The doubts were vague but definitely there.

The bus journey home was difficult (he was, after all, riding inside what would kill him tomorrow). He worked himself up into a state of panic. Sitting there he felt as though his arms and legs were disconnected from his body. He was a torso, and when his stop came he would float silently over to the doors and out into the night. His fellow passengers also seemed much smaller than they should — at least a head smaller — and when he looked at his window he didn't see the reflection of a sitting man; he saw himself lying on a bed, emaciated and purple, grey in places, his eyes closed, his mouth half-open. In less than twenty-four hours that's exactly how he would look, maybe much worse, maybe horribly disfigured.

The next thing he knew, it was Boxing Day and he was in hospital. The palms of his hands were badly grazed and he'd lost a fingernail. But that was pretty much it.

4

It's Monday morning and when Pete answers the door it's clear that his mood has darkened considerably since Friday. For the first fifteen minutes it's almost impossible to engage with him. He keeps walking about, picking things up and putting them down again. His breath smells of stale alcohol, and I get a whiff of it each time he passes by.

I cut straight to it and ask if it was him at the studio on Saturday. He doesn't exactly deny it, says he sort of remembers going over there but can't be one hundred per cent sure.

'How did you get the address?'

'I looked in my mind's eye and there it was.' He stops in front of the gas fire. 'I don't want to cook today. My back hurts. Come to the kitchen, though. There's something I want to show you.'

The last thing I expect it to be is Friday's cooking.

He takes the partially eaten shepherds pie out of the fridge and peels back the foil covering. Running his finger gently over the browned, grooved mashed potato, which ends about three quarters along the dish, he says,

'Look at that. Everything's still fine. Everyone's happy.'

'I'm not sure I know what you mean.'

'No?'

'No. You're going to have to help me out.'

'Don't you think it looks like a tiny ploughed field leading to a cliff? I've been looking at it all weekend. It looks like one of the places I visited with my parents the day of the crash. I remember it like it was yesterday. But then I would, wouldn't I?' He looks at me curiously. 'I wonder where you were that day.'

'I've no idea. What would I have been back then, five?'

'I wonder what you were doing. The exact moment the van hit us. Maybe playing with an Action Man, or drawing. I saw you in a vision once. You were wearing a home-knitted purple jumper. You used to have a jumper like that, didn't you?'

'Yes,' I say, a little unnerved, and pretty certain I would have never told him something so obscure.

'I wonder what happened to it. I wonder if it still exists in a material sense. I can almost see it somewhere, in a landfill, the sleeve sticking out from under a mountain of rubbish, food tins, soil and broken plates. I could tell you all sorts of things about yourself if you'd like me to. I should do it for a living, like Derren Brown. It's fascinating, don't you think, that things like that can be going on for one person, terrible things, a car crash, a dying mother, and somewhere else someone can be just playing?'

'Yes,' I say. 'It is.'

A sneer curls his lip. 'Don't pretend you care.'

'I'm not. I do care.'

'No you don't. You're just doing a job. You get paid to pretend to be my friend.'

I make a cup of tea and we sit down to watch TV. This seems to cheer him up for a while, but then he shows me the rent statement he's received informing him that he's £2,468 in arrears. Also, DLA have written to him to say there's a problem with his recent disability benefits claim form. I call them and they tell me that two questions haven't been answered satisfactorily: 2a. Do you have savings over £10,000? And 7c. Are you pregnant? Finally, I get them to agree on a plan of action. A new form will be sent to us, we should go over it and answer all the questions, the claim will then be reprocessed, all payments backdated.

The next call I make is to arrange a payment plan for his Littlewood's catalogue debt.

'Don't let Iris order anything else.'

He nods and picks up a light blue envelope. 'This came, too.'

I take the envelope from him and open it. It's an invitation to the coffee morning at Lady Gomm.

'I'm not going,' he says. 'So don't even bother asking.'

'Why? You used to like it, when Sarah worked there.'

'I've moved on. Things change. I'm not lonely anymore. And it's depressing. All day centres are.'

'She might pop in for a visit,' I tell him, but this is a white lie; Sarah's actually leaving for Devon later, when she's finished at the hospice. She heads there every once in a while to recharge her batteries. In some ways she knows what's good for her.

He doesn't take the bait, doesn't bat an eyelid, because of course he's right; day centres are God-awful places and I'm glad I no longer have to set foot in them. The days do anything *but* centre you. They pass in a haze of dominoes, DVDs, card games and tabloids, and leave you wanting only to do one thing — sleep the deepest sleep.

During my first weeks as a support worker, I did one day a week at Lady Gomm. I started up an art group. Pete was the first member. Fresh out of hospital and topped up with antidepressants, you'd rarely see him without a 00 paintbrush behind his ear. He was unstoppable. Bristling with energy. Week in week out he'd paint these small pictures of potatoes. Don't be fooled, they were beautiful and strangely moving, some of the most interesting paintings I've seen. Always on small boards, about the size of a paperback, his potatoes were fleshy, pinky-yellow, full of lumps and bumps, and they loomed up at you from a dark background like ghostly faces. What did he have to say about them? Not much; he didn't have to. He'd say, 'It's insane to give a potato so much attention, so that's exactly what I do.'

We head to the bathroom to weigh him. Fifty-seven kilos. One kilo more than last week.

'Good,' I say. 'Keep it up.'

Back in the kitchen we chat about this and that for a while. Then I make some toast, which he eats half a slice of. I wash the dishes while he watches TV, and as I'm vacuuming the hall I notice that at some point over the weekend he's secured the bedroom door with an almost comically oversized padlock.

I cut the power and walk to the living room. 'What's with Fort Knox?'

'A social worker came after you'd left on Friday and she walked straight in there

48

without even asking.'

'That's not right.'

'No it's not. My room's my business. I don't want people barging in there whenever they feel like it. It's the only private place I have.' He hauls himself up out of the chair. 'Come on. I'll see you out. It's 11. You go at 11.'

I get my things together and he walks me to the front door. As we stand on the doorstep a cream VW camper van drives by. 'I had a dream about one of those last night,' he says. 'How about that. It was exactly the same colour. Or maybe a bit lighter. Or it could have been white. I was with Iris on holiday, abroad. We were driving down a narrow street and a boy ran out from between two parked cars. Just before we hit him, I woke up. It was me.'

'Are you going to be okay? I could stay a bit longer.'

He nods, 'I'm fine.'

But there's a wild look in his eyes.

'Tomorrow, then. Lady Gomm?'

'Don't push it,' he says. 'I'll think about it.'

★   ★   ★

It's just gone 12.30 when I arrive at the hospice. I sign in at reception and take

49

the stairs up to the third floor. I never use the lifts here. I prefer to remind myself that I still have strength in my legs.

Clare's downgrade from hospital to hospice happened three months ago. And three months before that she was still living in South Africa, sick but determined to gather as much material as possible for her anthropology PhD. She's had pretty much everything there is to have — chemo, radiotherapy, X-rays, MRI scans, blood tests, her lungs drained and the lining stapled — everything but what she should have had, preventative surgery.

Her illness, like my mother's, is exhausting and relentless. But I've grown to like her.

At the top of the stairs I turn right and head for her room. I need to tread carefully. The urge to crack a pressure release joke is suddenly upon me.

I adopt an earnest expression and enter her room.

Sarah's sitting on the bed next to her sister's swollen legs. Clare, jaundiced, a purple crocheted skullcap covering her bald head, forces a smile. 'Hi.'

'Hi,' I say.

Sarah looks tired. 'Hi,' she says. 'How was Pete?'

'Not good. On a downer and telling me

weird things about myself. He spooked me a little today, to be honest.'

'What kind of things?'

'That I used to draw and play with Action Men.'

Clare frowns sceptically and snorts out a short laugh. 'You and every other boy.'

'And about a purple jumper I used to have.'

'I have a purple jumper.' She looks at Sarah. 'Don't you have a purple jumper?'

Sarah nods but looks a little wary.

'Yes,' I say. 'It might sound ridiculous. But there was something unnerving about it. On Friday he said he'd had a vision of something happening to me, something life changing.'

'Does he use psychic powers to speak with the dead?' Clare cuts in dryly. 'Keep him close. If there's anything you've forgotten to say to me, you'll need him once they wheel me out of here.'

'We were about to do some drawing,' Sarah says in an attempt to steer us away from doom and gloom. 'I'll draw you. Clare's drawing me. You can draw her.'

'Okay,' I say.

Paper is handed out and I look around for something hard to lean on. I remove the plate, cup and glass from Clare's tray and put all three on the shelf next to her sink. Pretty soon there's silence except for the scratch of pencils.

Sarah rubs something out and brushes aside the paper crumbs. I study Clare, my hand moves and a faint outline of her face appears before me. I scribble the knit of the skullcap and then blur some of the stitches with my thumb. The blurring weakens the drawing, so I ask Sarah for the rubber. Clare gasps, wide-eyed, when it's thrown over. 'Don't do that in here,' she says. 'This equipment is all that's keeping me alive.'

'Have you eaten today?' I ask her.

'I'm not one of your whateveryoucallthems — your patients.'

'I was just asking.'

'No I haven't. But *I* have an excuse.' She gestures at Sarah. 'What's hers? She hasn't eaten either. Anyone would think it was a skinny competition.' She circles her thumb and forefinger around her bicep and touches them together. 'There,' she says. 'Beat that.'

Sarah smiles sadly and looks my way. 'How's it going?'

'Okay. Not bad. Let's see yours.'

'Not yet. I need a few more minutes.'

Clare slaps her hand down on her pad. 'If you're going to keep moving, I'm wasting my time. How am I supposed to draw you when you keep moving?'

Sarah apologises, her head goes back down, and as I watch her scratch away at her paper, I wonder what things would be like for the two of us if we'd met under different circumstances.

People often assume we've been together for much longer than six months. They say we give off that impression. Maybe it's because we were plunged straight into the meat and potatoes of our relationship instead of having had time to play around with a starter. No happy-go-lucky honeymoon period for us. Our early dates were visits to hospitals, chemists, and health food shops to buy supplements, goji berries and different types of seaweed for Clare. When we weren't doing that we were working or driving up the M6 in Sarah's Mini to visit my dying mother. We probably moved in together too quickly, but it seemed like a good idea at the time. I feel cheated, and although Sarah hasn't admitted it, she probably feels the same way. Cancer, the thing we had in common and were glad to be able to talk about, has ended up being the thing I'd willingly sweep under the carpet, if I could only find one big enough.

Sarah came to the opening of an exhibition of mine. That's how we met. No-one I knew had invited her; she said she'd received a flyer by email. We got talking, we got drunk, and she told me about Clare's illness and her work for Open Door. For the last four years she'd managed the day centre. Her job made her life feel meaningful and she needed it to at the moment. She was a keen swimmer — in all weathers — loved salsa, green and grey together, Danish crime dramas, and one of her favourite quotes was by Kate Moss: 'Nothing tastes as good as skinny feels.'

Nobody could say I wasn't warned.

By the end of the evening we'd exchanged numbers and Sarah had convinced me that I should apply for a job where she worked. She said I was exactly the kind of person mental health charities were looking for — sensitive, thoughtful, one of life's strugglers. (I took this as a compliment whether it was meant as one or not.)

We met up again two days later. And from that point on there was something almost hard sell about the way she pursued me. She made all the phone calls, arranged where to meet, suggested things to do, even gave me a stack of books about cancer that she said would help me face up to my mother's imminent death. She was at the wheel, and I wasn't used to being the passenger. But I have to admit it, I was flattered.

Sarah is a very attractive woman. She has shoulder length black hair and the poise of an athlete — a very straight back and broad shoulders. People tend to watch her when she walks into a room, women just as much as men. She also has style. The evening we met, she had a grey scarf wrapped around her neck and hair. I liked that. I'm aware there are probably sounder reasons for wanting to be with someone, but if asked what hooked me in that evening, I'd say it was that — the scarf around the hair as well as the neck. That and her very light green eyes. And her soft, deep voice.

She has stopped drawing and is doing her best to sit still. But her best isn't good enough. Clare, clearly unhappy, sighs heavily and drops the pastel into her lap. 'This is awful,' she says bitterly.

'Show me,' I say.

'No.'

Sarah leans forward. 'Can *I* see?'

'No. It's your fault that it *is* awful. You keep moving.' She folds her arms. 'Well, since you already *have* moved, I suppose we might as well see the one you've done of *him*. Is it ready for a viewing yet? Are we allowed?'

Sarah smiles sheepishly and turns her drawing towards us.

There is a likeness. Sarah draws well. Pencil outlines, my face blue, my stubble and short hair suggested with a darker blue, some dark browns, some black.

Clare laughs wickedly. 'He looks like the devil.'

'The devil can't be blue,' I point out.

'The devil can be whatever colour he likes. When we eventually meet, and I'm pretty sure we will, *I* won't argue with him if he's chosen to be pink with green spots.'

Sarah turns the drawing around again and studies it. 'I'm quite pleased with it,' she says. She places it on her lap and adds more blue stubble. Then she pauses, listening. 'Isn't that your phone?' She slides my bag over with her foot.

I take out my phone and look at the screen. *Pete calling*.

I stand and move towards the door. 'Sorry. I should probably get this.' I step out into the empty corridor. An echoey cough comes from one of the rooms. Food is scraped off a plate in the kitchen. I quietly close the door behind me. 'Pete. Everything okay?'

'I need to talk to you.'

'We'll have to keep it short. I'm a bit busy. I'm — '

'At the hospice. I know. I'm outside in the car park. Are you coming down or shall I go?'

'Give me a minute,' I say.

I head down the stairs intending to be angry, outraged at what could now surely be classed as stalking. But when I see how especially small and alone he looks I soften. As I approach, he attempts a smile, but it's fairly obvious he's been crying.

'Pete, what are you doing here? And how did you know how to find me?'

'I have a question for you,' he sniffs. 'An important one. Do you think machines will ever really *know* what they can do, besides just being able to do them?'

'I have no idea. I can't say it's something I've given much thought to.' A line from Springsteen's 'Born to Run' comes to me — *at night we ride the mansions of glory in suicide machines* — and I picture something enormous and elaborate hiding away behind the newly padlocked bedroom door, some crude Heath Robinson contraption with tubes and syringes, or maybe a gun on a tripod with a long string tied to the trigger.

'I think they will,' he says. 'But that's not what I wanted to ask you. I've been looking at that book you left me. Hopper.'

'Good,' I say, relieved to be back on normal ground. 'What do you think of his work?'

'I like it. That painting of his, *High Noon*, the one of the woman in the doorway of the white house. Did you know he made a cardboard model of the house, so that he could put it out in the sun and study the effects of light and shade?'

'No, I didn't.'

'He wanted to get things right. He was a perfectionist.'

'I can't really do this now, Pete,' I say, and I look up at Clare's window to see Sarah looking down at us. She waves. Pete waves back. 'She hasn't told you,' he asks. 'Has she?'

'Told me what?'

'It doesn't matter. Obviously not. And there's no point in quizzing her. She won't go behind my back. She's not like that. She gave me her word, and I trust her.'

'I have no idea what you're talking about, Pete, but I think you'd best go home. I need to get back up there.' I look up again. Sarah has now disappeared, and I wonder if she's on her way down to meet us.

'Okay,' he says. 'One last thing. What do you think happened to Hopper's model? Do you think someone owns it? Some art collector?'

'I've no idea.'

'Do you really think he made it because of light? That's what the book says, but it's just a book, isn't it, a book written by someone who thinks they understand the workings of someone else's mind. No-one ever really knows anyone else's mind, not fully. Take my word for it. People don't even know their own minds because every day a mind discovers something new, so technically speaking it's not the same mind. Like the thing about a river. Heraclitus. You never step into the same river twice. It's not the same river. It's moved on. Do you think there might have been another reason why he made a model?'

'I have no idea. It's possible. We can chat about it some other time. But not now.'

'Forget it,' he says. 'Will she really be there tomorrow? At Lady Gomm?'

'Sarah? Yes. Maybe.'

'Okay.'

And just like that, he turns and walks away.

When I get back up to Clare's room, Sarah is back at the window. Clare is colouring in a large area of pink and seems to be enjoying herself. She looks up. 'Ah, he's back.'

'Sorry about that,' I say, and I sit down.

Sarah turns from the window. 'Everything okay?'

'Not really.'

'Why, what's wrong?'

'How did he know how to find this place. Did you tell him?'

'No. When?'

'I don't know.'

'I don't see him. Maybe your address book fell out of your bag at his flat. Maybe he rooted through it. Who knows.'

'Let's talk about it later.'

'Oh, don't mind me,' Clare says sarcastically. 'Should I leave the room so you can share your little secrets? Sarah's good at keeping secrets, always has been, all her life. Isn't that right, Sarah?'

Sarah doesn't answer.

Clare turns to me again. 'What part of me were you drawing? Before you went out.'

'Your head. Your face,' I tell her.

'What part of me are you going to draw now?'

'Your mouth.'

'Don't make me look ugly and miserable. And don't make my cheeks look puffy. I don't know why I even agreed to this in the first place. I hate being stared at.' She narrows her eyes at her drawing and then slaps the pad and sighs heavily.

'Now what's wrong?' I ask her.

'Her head's too small.' She holds up the bright pastel drawing for us to see. The pink of Sarah's t-shirt is exactly the right colour, and her head is only a little smaller than it's supposed to be.

'It's great,' I say.

Clare scowls. 'It isn't. She looks stupid. And I've made her look fat.'

Sarah's eyes widen noticeably at this.

I put down my pencil. 'Right. That's it. If I

do anymore I'll spoil it.' I turn the drawing towards Sarah.

'Auuuh,' she says. 'It's beautiful. The eyelashes are lovely.'

Clare tuts. '*I'd* quite like to see it too. It is of me, after all.'

I angle it towards her and hope for the best. 'What do you think? Do you like it?'

★　★　★

Twenty minutes later the hospice doors glide closed behind us. Halfway across the car park, Sarah touches my arm and stops me. 'I have something to ask you,' she says.

'Okay.'

'I keep bingeing on rice cakes. I'm sure you've noticed. Do you think we could maybe not buy them for a while?'

I can't help but look baffled. 'Are you joking?'

'No.'

'Rice cakes?'

'Yes. It would help me, and I could do with some at the moment.'

'Fine,' I shrug. 'No more rice cakes. Now can I ask you something?'

'Sure,' she says.

'Pete asked if you'd 'told me'. What did he mean?'

'I don't know.'

'Sarah, I don't believe you. What if it's something serious? I'm his key worker. I know you've known him longer than I have, but that's not the point. If there is something you know, you should probably tell me. You know how vulnerable he is at the moment. He could kill himself. He could kill me. That would be pretty life changing.'

'He won't. He won't do either of those.'

'You're sure about that.'

'Yes. I've worked with people who are on the edge. And he isn't. Not yet.'

'Not yet?'

She shakes her head confidently.

I study her expression and can tell she isn't telling the truth.

'So,' she says. 'We're agreed on the rice cakes, yeah? We won't buy them for a while. You okay with that?'

Amazed she's still pursuing this after I already agreed to her terms, I lose my temper. 'Do you know rice cakes are mostly made from air, Sarah. You probably use more calories eating one than there is *in* one. Like celery. So tell me, where's the problem?'

'We're not on the same path,' she says sadly. 'When we first met, I thought we were, but I was obviously wrong.'

'We don't have to share everything. You're

obviously not prepared to.'

'You should probably let that drop now, David,' she sighs. 'Because if you remember, I already told you that I have no idea what he meant. Are you going to keep on asking? It won't make me suddenly understand what you're talking about.' She unfolds her arms and looks at her nails, and we stand in silence for a while.

'Two weeks,' I finally say. 'No, make it three. Is that long enough?'

'For what?'

'The rice cake ban.'

'Forget it,' she says. 'If you're going to be sarcastic. Go ahead. Fill the cupboards. Sweet ones, salted ones, savoury ones, Marmite flavoured ones. Get the lot.' She shakes her head and points her car key at me. 'You know where the word sarcastic comes from, David? It comes from a Greek word. It means to tear flesh. That's what you do. You're good at it, always have been. Mr nice guy with a knife up his sleeve. That's you. Me, I'm just weak and pathetic.'

'I never said you were weak.'

'You don't have to. I know you think I am. And you, well, you're perfect.'

We are still alone in the car park. I no longer want to be here. I want to be up a mountain, on a horse, in the sea, hang-gliding over a lush green valley. I take a breath. 'I've agreed to what you want, Sarah. I won't buy them if it will help. Now, let's go.'

She stares towards her car. A tear rolls down her cheek and ducks under her jawbone. I put my arms around her and hold her for a while.

She wipes at her eyes with the back of her sleeve and takes a step back. 'So, what else did Pete say?'

'Just some crazy stuff. About all kinds of things. I hope he's not coming off his meds again.'

'Maybe get him to take them while you're with him.'

'I'll suggest it and see what he says.'

Sarah nods and wipes her eyes again.

A coach load of pensioners drives slowly by, and a few of them look uneasily at the St Catherine's Hospice sign, then at us — the arguing couple — and I wonder if it makes them feel any better for having seen us. I don't feel sorry for them for being old. I envy them. Careers. Marriage. Children. All of this is behind them, ticked off the list. Life is now just a series of outings and packed lunches, book clubs, museum and Cathedral tours. Not something to be sniffed at.

A woman enters the car park and heads for reception. Sarah waits until the automatic doors have closed behind her before continuing. 'Can I ask you something else?' she says.

I nod.

'Have you ever been completely satisfied with me?'

'Where the hell did that suddenly come from?'

'You don't think I'm enough for you,' she says. 'You say I am, but I know you're not telling the truth. You'd prefer it if I wasn't just someone with a job. You'd be happier if I was an artist or musician, something like that.'

'You're wrong. I think that would be awful.'

'Oh yeah? And why's that?'

'Because I think artists are probably hard to live with, and yes I include myself in that.'

'One day you'll realise that I was just trying to help you.'

'Help me? Help me with what?'

'Never mind. It doesn't matter. Just remember we had this conversation.'

5

The idea that madness and genius are close cousins isn't a particularly new one. Einstein could barely take care of himself because his head was so crammed full of ideas. Pollock, Rothko, Hemmingway, Virginia Woolf, Tchaikovsky, Kurt Cobain — none of them able to find meaning in life outside their work. The world may still speculate as to why they chose to end their lives — plain old depression, the death of a father, back pain, closet homosexuality — but that's all it is and always will be. I agree with Pete. No-one *can* ever truly understand the workings of someone else's mind.

They say the brain is like the ocean — largely unexplored and pretty much doing its own thing. Unpredictable. Baffling. A force to be reckoned with. Why is it that I can remember random but specific moments from childhood? Sitting on the carpet drawing a horse while my mother irons. Helping my dad paint the outside of the house while 'Walking on the Moon' by The Police plays on the radio. And yet I can sometimes barely remember how I spent yesterday. Maybe the brain is more like a smartphone. Fast and powerful when new, sluggish when too many apps are up and running.

There are artists I know who feign eccentricity and talk in impenetrable language. I've never wanted to be like that, and I avoid them at all costs. I'd describe myself as intelligent and articulate but essentially down to earth. Most of the artists I spend time with are like tradesmen — carpenters, plumbers or builders. They have a skill, a handful of ideas, and a sound knowledge of their materials. They go to the studio each morning, boil the kettle, put on the radio, change into their overalls and get down to whatever it is they do.

I have a friend up north who builds climbing walls for a living. It's fascinating going to his workshop. It smells of pear drops (cellulose thinners) and damp sand. Whenever I see him we end up having the same conversation. He asks me what the difference is between what he does and what I do, what it is that makes what I do art and what he does a product. For ease I opt out and tell him that I have no idea. Back in my art school days I could have argued it out with him for hours. I would have wanted to. I'd have told him that it was all about context, could have name-checked people like Duchamp or Andre. The whole 'ready made' thing.

Put a urinal or some bricks in a gallery and it becomes art. Bingo! The thing is, and I say this in all seriousness, all of that seemed like bollocks to me from the start, and it still does. I just make paintings. I build a frame, stretch canvas over it, paint rabbit skin glue on the canvas to make it tighten. Then I start a painting. It's that simple.

At art school I was the same way. I just wanted to get on with the work. I wasn't interested in trying to shock or creating a look. Green or pink hair. Odd shoes (one black Converse, one red). Glasses with the cellophane wrappers from Quality Street glued to the lenses (don't ask). Used tampons passed off as sculpture. None of this was for me. If I'd turned up one day with Pete and a few more of Open Door's clients I'd have been hailed as the new messiah. Genuine strangeness is, I've come to realise, on the inside rather than the outside.

I'd have tutorials with a lecturer called Paul Hampton. Very Downton Abbey — lambs-wool jumpers, light brown cords — and about a head shorter than me. It was obvious that he didn't like me. I was too working class. He'd come into my space and look at something I'd taped to the wall — a napkin, for example, with a scribbled sketch on it. He'd then start talking in great length about the napkin instead of the painting I'd been labouring over for the last two weeks, the 'masterpiece' that had come about through sheer hard labour. The thing is, he was actually right. If something is interesting, it's interesting. Full stop. It doesn't matter if it took a few seconds or a year to make it.

He once looked at another piece of my work — a construction I'd built out of bits of wood I'd salvaged and painted on — and said that it demonstrated a 'sophisticated spatial sensitivity'. I was flattered but asked him to explain in more detail what he meant. 'Like a lorry driver,' he said. 'The way he can reverse his vehicle with an instinctive knowledge of its bulk and size. The way he can almost close his eyes and do it without any danger of hitting anything.'

He went on like this for a while, but all I heard was something along the lines of: you are common, should stick with wood and tools and what you already know, and never, I repeat *never* get ideas above your station. Painting is something you would be wise to leave alone etc, etc . . .

The next time I saw him he'd just returned from a trip to the Lake District. He'd gone there to paint watercolours. I could picture him in a valley wearing a smock and beret. Flask of coffee. Packed lunch. One of those palettes with the thumb hole in it. He said he'd had a terrible experience. He'd set up in a quarry just outside Grasmere and was about to get started when he heard a hammer drill echoing down from above. Drrrrrrrrrr . . . Drr . . . Drr . . . Drrrrrrrrrrr . . . The ambience was shattered, the whole trip ruined. Climbers were putting tie off bolts in the rock face. I mean, really! . . .

I was up north faster than you can say Black and Decker. 'I need you to show me how to make a climbing wall,' I told my friend.

He showed me how to make latex moulds to cast the bolt-on handholds in, taught me how to mix resin — two parts solution, one part hardener. I learned how to shape the wall panels using fibreglass matting coated with 2pac glue and sand to create the appearance of rock.

The piece turned out to be the talking point of the department and the second year exhibition. I'd titled it *You Drive Me Up the Fucking Wall, Paul*. Someone bought it for a decent amount of money. I forget who it was. I know who it wasn't.

Pricing is the one thing I'm glad I don't have to deal with. I was never any good at it. Ironic that Price is my name.

My gallery deals with that side of things.

They'll phone and tell me they've sold something. Then they send me my 50%. Yes, it is a big chunk, don't think I don't know it, but it's worth it not to have to do it all yourself.

About six years ago I met a couple at an open studio weekend. They bought a small painting of a dead bird with a broken wing lying on a carpet below a window — *Departure Lounge*. They took one of my business cards, and a week later the wife called to ask if I'd consider a commission. I told her I'd think about it and get back to her in a few days time.

It turned out that she wanted to give her husband a print for his birthday. An etching. She wanted it to be personal and something only he would ever have, a one-off. They'd lived in Vienna a few years ago, and the husband's favourite book was *The Little Prince* (bit strange for a grown man, but each to their own). If I could do an etching incorporating these two things, that would be just perfect.

I worked on the plate for two weeks. Etching is great. You feel like a scientist. You have a metal plate and you roll on a kind of warmed up resin, which hardens when it cools. You then draw into it, dip it in acid and the acid eats into the line. You clean the plate off, roll on ink, and make a print from it.

I went to the woman's flat in Knightsbridge to show her a sample print. I felt like a fish out of water there. The hallway had a full-sized snooker table in it, and the sitting room was big enough to play five-a-side football in. We sat on one of the three available sofas, and when I slipped the metal plate from the hessian bag I'd had specially made, she let out a little gasp. 'Oh,' she said. 'How beautiful.'

She loved the print and told me I needn't bother making another. It was perfect, and she loved the idea that it was the first and last in existence (I didn't tell her I'd already printed off three others). I signed and numbered it for her: *David Price. 1/1. 2007* — and then it was time to have the money conversation.

'We never discussed how much,' she said.

'No.'

'My fault. Silly of me.'

'Don't worry about it. I should have said something.'

She got out her cheque book and a tortoiseshell fountain pen. I swear to God. I was half expecting her to open up a drawer and bring out a cut glass inkwell. 'Okay,' she said. 'Fire away.'

I went off on one. 'Well, with this print, the

thing is, as you know, there's only one, and there only ever will be, because you own the plate now, and unless you decide to have another one printed off, you'll never walk into someone's house anywhere in the world and see this image, your image, or hear of it for sale, if I ever make the big time. You can even destroy the plate if you like, or lock it in a safe, whatever. The bag is made of hessian, by the way. I had it specially sourced from — '

She gently put her hand on my forearm. Her other was still poised with the fountain pen. 'How much do I owe you?' she said.

The thing is, I hadn't given it much thought. I'd been so wrapped up in making sure I did a good job (very working class — Paul would have been proud) I'd neglected the money side of things completely. Not for a minute, on my way over there, in my un-ironed shirt and slightly too-short pin-striped trousers, had it crossed my mind.

'£300,' I said off the top of my head.

She looked shocked. Offended almost. I think she wanted to pay more, much more, so that she could show off at dinner parties. She shrugged and wrote the cheque. I could prob-ably have said five grand and she wouldn't have batted an eyelid. Maybe even ten.

6

My bike is locked to the drainpipe outside Pete's local, The Blue Anchor on Half Moon Lane. I've only ever passed by this place but inside I find it's exactly as I pictured it: scratched tables, torn upholstery, two scabby pub dogs and three overweight women in vests eating Chinese takeaway.

Pete rushes over when he sees me appear in the doorway. We sit down and he apologises for appearing at the hospice. He doesn't know what came over him.

For the next ten minutes he babbles on about fire, over excitedly quoting from a Radio 4 programme he listened to about the unstable nature of materials. Holding his hand as though there's an invisible gun in it, his thumb performs a strange ritualistic touching of the tips of each finger in turn. Brow furrowed, he places an unlit cigarette on the table. 'Do you know anything about wood?'

'Yes,' I say. 'A bit. Why?'

'Wood likes to oxidise. It has a memory. It knows it can burst into flames.' He lifts up his shirt and places both palms against his flesh, appearing to be listening for something through them (I haven't seen this mannerism before and should probably write it up later). He picks up the cigarette again. 'Someone on the programme once worked in a sawmill, and one day a barrel of sawdust began smoking for no reason. When they opened it up, they found the fire had started in the *centre* of the sawdust. Not at the edges, or the top, but the centre. Amazing. How could sawdust just set itself alight like that if it didn't know it could?'

'I have no idea.'

'And petrol floats on water. Did you know that?'

'Yes.'

'Like on puddles.'

'Like on puddles.'

'You can probably set fire to it. Make water burn.'

'Yes,' I say. 'I imagine so.'

'But you'd need a fair amount.' He stands up, nodding to himself. 'Toilet.' And he walks away.

I begin flicking through a copy of *Metro* someone has left behind. *Metro* is a decent read. Interesting articles. Good film and art reviews. Low on tittle-tattle. Quirky people stories. I come across one about a man who makes art out of food. So far he's made Van Gogh's *Sunflowers* out of cheese, a Mondrian from different coloured cake, and a Salvador

Dali from bacon, sausages, and various other meats.

I'm no fan of Dali. I find his work silly. But I have visited his house in Cadaques. Sarah and I went there by accident not long after we met.

Our intention was to take a long weekend in Barcelona. Clare had just come back from South Africa and was already in hospital. My mother was in the middle of chemo. We needed to get away from illness and live a little, wash the smell of it from our skin.

For two days we snooped around The Gothic Quarter, saw Gaudi's (still) unfinished Church of the Holy Family (ugly, in my opinion), drank mulled wine at a Christmas street market and ate in restaurants along The Passeig de Gracia. We switched off our phones and left them at the hotel. Not once did we mention — or even think about — our lives back home.

Until we decided to hire a car and drive down the coast.

I have to admit it, Dali's house is pretty impressive. Perched precariously on the cliffside, it's surprisingly modern — simple and white on the outside, huge floor to ceiling windows overlooking the harbour. Dali designed it himself, apparently, but he locked the door and simply walked away when his wife Gala died. When he died seven years later, he left the house to the Spanish government and they opened it up to the public.

Out back was a swimming pool shaped like a cock and balls. A nearby sign informed us that Dali had always liked the idea of swimming up the shaft in the same way a sperm does. Swimming for him was symbolic of life itself. I took out my pad, made a sketch, and came up with a half decent title.

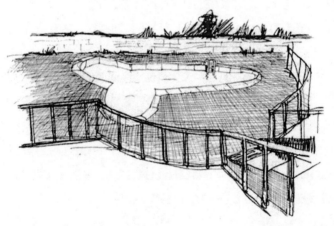

Gene Pool
Biro on paper 170 x 120 cm

His upstairs studio was tiny. But in the floor was a long slit which larger canvasses could be slipped up through, worked on, then winched back down again. A small blank canvas was set up on an easel. The floor was very clean, not a paint spill or splash in sight. Dried worms of colour were cracking open on a palette.

What was surprising about the rest of the house was how tidy most of the rooms were. I'd expected chaos. Had someone tidied up? Apparently not. The place was exactly, so we were told, just as he'd left it. A half-spherical room. A long galley kitchen with polished copper pans. A small room just for shoes. A dining room with a wine rack in the fireplace. A black bathroom with a dedication written on the wall in white: *For my Gala, Queen in death of Lunar light on water.*

Downstairs, next to the heavy, wooden front door was a circular pin-board of photographs, mostly of Dali and Gala with famous people they'd met at one time or another — Marilyn Monroe, Fidel Castro, Elizabeth Taylor and Richard Burton. And at this point something happened to me, something I still think of as a kind of mini epiphany.

I often get the feeling, when looking at photographs in someone's house, that I might see one of someone I know. I had the feeling then; I almost expected to recognise a handful of familiar places and faces: Dali with an arm draped over the shoulders of my parents; with an old teacher of mine; shaking the hand of Matt or Michael at the timberyard where I buy wood for my canvas stretchers; dancing with the girl from the Baskets Only checkout in Tesco. I scanned the photos, and obviously this didn't happen. What did, though, was this: As my gaze settled on a snap in which the Dalis were standing next to a camel and smiling broadly into the camera, something dawned on me, and I turned to Sarah.

'Look at the two of them,' I said. 'They're just like everyone else. Human beings. Flesh, blood and funny hairstyles.' Sarah nodded, though she did look a bit baffled. It didn't matter. I knew exactly what I meant. All the showy eccentricities aside — anteaters on leads, curled moustache, those eyes (one always wider than the other) — Dali was just a man, a man standing next to his smiling wife who would die before him. No matter what he does, who he knows, or how rich he is, that will still happen, and there isn't a thing he can do to stop it.

That may not sound like much to write home about, certainly not much of an epiphany, but at the time it felt profound, significant in some way, a key moment in time. For me, the whole of life seemed to have been played out in the thirty minutes I'd spent in that house, much more of a life than I'd lived up until that point. One minute there we were, sperm heading for the egg, like Dali in his pool, the next we were nothing but a few carefully considered words on a bathroom wall.

'I actually think it might be one of the saddest photographs I've ever seen.'

Sarah frowned, surprised. 'Sad? Why? They look like they're having a great time.'

'Yes. But she'll eventually become senile and die. And look at him. He has no idea.'

'Him? What about her?'

'She could easily have lived without him. But he didn't do too well when she was gone. He lost the will to live, tried to kill himself a couple of times.'

'Sometimes I wish it was all over for Clare. I feel awful admitting that, but it's true. I know she'll die, but it's hard not knowing when. You know, not knowing how long things will drag on for?'

'Yes. I'm sure my dad does too, but he'd never be brave enough to admit it.'

Sarah sighed. 'When I was a kid, whenever someone told one of those *a man goes to the doctor and the doctor tells him he has six months to live* jokes, I used to believe that a doctor could really pin it down that accurately. You know, to the exact day. If I could have a superpower, that would be it. I fucking hate uncertainty.'

I walked out of that house and into the winter sunlight feeling galvanised. And I made a vow to myself that once back home I'd start a new series of paintings based on my parents life together.

None of this happened. When I switched on my phone back at Heathrow, there was a voicemail from my dad saying that I should probably head home as soon as possible. I was in Sarah's Mini and on the M6 that evening. Three days after that, my mother was dead.

⋆　⋆　⋆

Pete appears from around the corner, water spots dotting the front of his shirt.

'We should go and look at some art next week,' I say. 'Tate Modern maybe. The Rothko room. That will cheer us up.'

'I don't need cheering up. Drink?'

I shake my head. 'No thanks. I need to ask you something.'

He puts the unlit cigarette in his mouth. 'I'm going out for a smoke. No, okay, I'll go in a minute.' He sits down. 'Do you know why New York is called The Big Apple?'

I shake my head.

'Would you like to?'

'Go on. Why not?'

This is the last ramble I will allow him.

'There are a few theories. It might be because New York is apple shaped when seen from a plane. Or it could be because of a

French woman called Eve who had a brothel there — the girls were her little apples. The apple is a symbol of fertility, and apple juice contains acids which can help fight cancer. Apple pips contain cyanide though. If you eat enough of them, say a pint glass full, you could die. The man who invented the first computer killed himself by taking a bite out of an apple he'd injected with cyanide. He was a fan of fairy tales, especially Snow White and the Seven Dwarves. The Apple Mac logo is a tribute to him. The other — '

'Pete,' I say, cutting him off mid-flow. 'What was all that about earlier?'

'All what?'

'Sarah having something to tell me.'

'I don't know what you mean.'

'At the hospice. You asked if she'd 'told me'. Told me what?'

'I don't remember saying that.' He gazes wistfully off into the distance. 'I remember being at the hospice but don't remember why. I don't remember the journey back either. I was there, then I was here. There's nothing in between. Sorry for turning up like that. I think it's the medication.'

'You're taking it?'

'Yes.'

'You sure?'

'Positive.'

'It might not be such a great idea to keep things from me. I am only here to help you. You know that, right?'

He nods.

'Good. If you change your mind, and you'd like to tell me, let me know.'

'I will. I mean if I remember that there is something, I definitely will.'

'And how are you feeling now?'

'Optimistic.'

'About what?'

'Everything.'

'Good. How's Iris?'

'She's okay. Her and John are getting married next month.'

'I thought they already were married.'

'They're not.'

'How do you feel about that?'

'I'm pleased for her. Whatever makes her happy. I want her to be happy.'

'She's lucky to have you as a friend, Pete. I hope she realises that. What do the two of you get up to when you go out?'

'Go to cafés and smoke our heads off.'

'Does it bother you when I mention her?'

'No.'

'You seem a bit jumpy when I do. You always have a quick comeback.'

'You don't like her.'

'I don't think she always tells the truth.

And I know you'll never admit it, but we know she's stolen money from you in the past.'

'You don't know her. And she'd never do that. She gossips a bit, but that's hardly a crime.'

For the first time since I arrived, he looks me in the eyes. 'How come you never talk about the people in your life? Boundaries?'

'That's right.'

'Don't you ever feel like talking about your parents?'

'My parents? Why my parents?'

'Because they're your family.'

'Like I said, I can't — '

He waves a hand at me. 'Don't worry. I don't need to know. The past is the past. You're an only child, right. Am I allowed to ask that?'

'Yes you are. And yes I am.'

'Did you never wish for a brother or sister?'

'Sometimes.'

'I was glad I had my half-sister. We were close once, but she still blames me for the crash.'

'I don't understand. How does that make sense?'

'She says we wouldn't have been in the car if it hadn't been for me.'

'Why not?'

'We were on our way to a pub for a special lunch. They had something to tell me. My mum was turned around in her seat talking to me. My dad looked over his shoulder and smiled. That was when my sister screamed and I saw the van on our side of the road. Apparently they were going to tell me I was adopted. Like I hadn't already worked it out for myself.'

7

I'm sitting at my kitchen table looking at letter #2 — a poem in handwritten Gothic script. It just arrived, and I'm pretty sure Pete is the author. Why he'd send it to me in the post, I have no idea.

> **Gliding to her destiny below**
> **Girl into woman**
> **Then a cry in the dark**
> **As two bright lights**
> **up-end the world,**
> **Bringing, eventually,**
> **An infant into being**
> **Who is not the chosen one.**

8

My mother died just before midnight on the 19th of December. Me and my dad were sitting by her bed holding a hand each. I'd known all day that we were almost at the end. A sixth sense definitely comes to you when you need it.

It had rained for the last two days and my mother had joked that the coffin they carried her out in had better be waterproof. That had been her mood — defiantly upbeat. But then in the afternoon of the 19th her leg swelled up and she retreated back inside herself. I called out the nurse and she arrived within half an hour. She examined my mother and came back downstairs with a resigned smile on her face. Lymphoedema again. We should prepare ourselves. It wouldn't be long now.

I stayed with my mother from that point on, only leaving her to go off and make tea or to warm up soup. She slept mostly, but in the evening she perked up a little and read some of her book — Steven King's *The Stand*. She even ate a cheese sandwich and a lemon yoghurt.

Around 10 p.m. I was sitting by her bed,

flicking through a magazine, when I heard her close the book and put it on the bedside table. She looked at me. 'Do you know how I met your dad?'

I thought about it for a few seconds. Oddly enough, I couldn't remember. 'I don't think I do, no.'

'It's quite a story. Would you like to hear it?'

'If you're not too tired.'

'I met him at the barn on top of Rivington Pike,' she began. 'In 1973. They used to have a disco up there on a Saturday night. We'd go up there every week. We'd get a lift up, but the rule was we weren't allowed to travel home alone, there always had to be at least two of us. There was a cocky lad who was always asking me to dance, no matter how many times I'd said no. One night he offered to take me home but I told him that I already had a lift, which was true. When it came to the end of the night, me and my friend, Lynne, got in a car with four boys.'

'How old were you?'

'Nineteen? Twenty? We set off and the boys agreed to take us all the way home to Wigan, but they didn't know the way. Anyway, we were going down the hill, and the driver asked which way, and I said, 'straight across', but I meant he should stop first, obviously.

Well he didn't, and I could see this car approaching from the right. I closed my eyes, curled into a ball, crouched down and there was an almighty bang. We flipped over about three times.'

'You're joking.'

'Oh yes, three times, easily, right across the dual carriageway. We ended up upside down. I think a tree stopped us. I think we knocked it over.'

'I can't believe you survived that.'

'Well I did. We all did. There was dead silence for a while, and I could hear the car wheels spinning round. And then out of the darkness, Lynne said, 'Is everybody okay?' We all said yes and she asked if anybody was smoking, meaning, you know, because of the petrol. But nobody was.'

'You can remember all that?'

'I can, yes. And then we all got out of the car.'

'What about the car that hit you?'

'It was a youngish couple with a small boy. I think he was about eight or nine, poor little thing. I think the woman died.'

I can feel the hairs on the back of my neck standing on end thinking about this now. Every time I go over the story the same thing happens. A youngish couple with a small boy. The woman died. It's hard not to see the similarities between the two crashes, virtually impossible I'd say. It's an almost identical scenario. But no sister. If we hadn't been talking about a crash that happened two years before Pete was even born, I'd have been on the phone to my dad as soon as I'd read his file — *'Dad, you're not going to believe this . . . '*

'What happened next?'

'We got out and we were standing about in the road. I think someone had sent for the police by then, and I remember thinking there was something wrong with my shoulder.'

'I can't believe you were all okay.'

'I know. I think it was because there were so many of us in the car, how we were wedged in like sardines. Anyway, we were standing there and this car pulled up behind us, and the cocky lad who was always asking me to dance got out. He'd followed us down the hill.'

'Dad.'

'How did you guess?'

'Did you get married soon after?'

'Yes, very quickly, but things went wrong and we separated and only got back together again two years later.'

'Wow! I didn't know any of that. I suppose you must have been meant for each other.'

'I wouldn't say it was quite like that.' At this point she took my hand. 'I think I probably owe you an apology.'

'For what?'

'Everything. All the arguing when you were growing up. It wasn't fair on you.'

'There wasn't that much. Was there?'

'Well at least that's something,' she said. 'Some consolation that you don't even remember half of it. That makes me feel a bit better. Being a parent is hard, David. You make a mess of lots of things and get the odd bit right. You'll find that out for yourself one day. Soon, I hope. Sarah's a nice girl. A bit thin but nice. You should stick with her. I'm tired now. I need to sleep.'

She did. And she never woke up again.

She was carried downstairs and taken away in the middle of the night. The next thing I remember I was looking at the clock as I stuffed her bedding into the washing machine. It was 3 a.m. I took the dog for a long walk and cried for most of it.

The undertaker came to the house around midday to discuss the funeral arrangements. He showed us a laminated catalogue of coffins. My dad chose mid-range. As the details were written down I had to stop myself from blurting out, 'By the way, before we commit, is that one definitely waterproof?'

In the afternoon I drove to the chemist and handed over two carrier bags of medication to be disposed of safely. Then I took the Christmas tree down and packed the lights and decorations away.

9

Me and Pete are in our pyjamas. We are sitting on the kerb eating popcorn. It's dark, there's been a car accident, and we are watching the scene unfold. Two women lie in the road, one blonde, one dark haired. A man appears out of nowhere and begins walking towards the dark haired woman, sealing her fate as a mother. I look over at the blonde woman. She's face down, one of her legs bent at an impossible angle. She twitches, makes a gurgling noise, and is still. Her stint as a mother has just ended.

My ringtone jerks me awake. I stretch for my phone. It's Phil with some worrying news.

Late last night someone set fire to Iris' in-laws-to-be garden pond.

Petrol was poured on the water and lit. The heat smashed the glass patio doors. Plastic garden furniture melted. Plants were scorched. Whoever was responsible (no prizes for guessing who the number one suspect is) returned in the middle of the night and attempted to scrub a smoke-blackened Buddha statue clean. Two offerings were left at its decorative base: a bitten, pip-less half apple and two daffodils.

I hear Phil exhale smoke into the phone. 'Don't say anything when you go round to see him. See if he mentions it first. I'm not sure if the police have contacted him yet.'

'Okay,' I say. 'I'll be in touch.'

I go about my morning routine — tea, toasted bagel, splash face twice with cold water — wondering if I should have mentioned the fire and water conversation I had with Pete in the pub. Even if he's guilty (and let's face it, there's a fair chance he is) I'm pretty sure he won't be in any great hurry to confess. For the moment he's safe. How would anyone ever prove he was lying anyway? At times like this I suppose there are certain advantages to being him.

Q: Where were you last night between 11 p.m. and midnight?
A: Where I am every night, at home.
Q: Can anyone vouch for that?
A: No. I only have one friend and she was somewhere else.

I arrive at his flat at the usual time. But ten minutes later he still hasn't answered the door. I shout through the letter box, picturing him lying stiff and yellow on the bathroom floor in a pool of his own vomit. Is today the day?

His neighbour, Mrs Baldwin, a large black

woman, is on her hands and knees on the other side of the low dividing fence. Most of the time she's fairly civil, but I doubt she approves of Pete's drinking and occasional shouting, or much likes the idea that he's registered under the Mental Health Act. Scrubbing her doorstep she hums what sounds like a hymn. She drops the brush into her yellow plastic bucket, and when she leans back to stretch her spine she glances up at me, not for the first time.

'Nice morning,' I say.

She forces a smile and drags the bucket closer to the wall. She dips the brush and shakes off the excess. Scrubbing is resumed, circular swishing that sends small waves of foam over the step's edge. Her skirt is damp in her lap. There are bubbles at the hem.

By half past nine I'm beginning to worry. Again I peer through the letter box. The hall is dark, the kitchen full of sunlight. Face pressed against the bay window, I repeat my scan of the living room. The TV is off, the room as tidy as usual. Not a dirty plate or cup in sight.

Gripping the fence with both hands I grin amicably. Mrs Baldwin lazily comes back onto her haunches and looks up at me, both eyebrows raised.

'I don't suppose you could let me through

to the back of your house,' I say. 'I need to climb the fence and get into Pete's garden. Have you seen him at all this morning?'

'No,' she says flatly.

'Could you let me through?'

She wipes her brow. 'I don't have a key.'

I look at her closed front door. 'Okay,' I say, confused. 'I see.'

She shrugs, leans forward, and begins scratching at a small area of the step with her fingernail.

I walk back onto the street, watching her, and although she's feigning total involvement with the step, I know she's keeping an eye on me too. I open her neighbour's gate and walk up to the front door. I ring the bell and wait. No-one home. I try the next house. Then the next. Then three houses on the other side. Nothing. I return to her gate.

'Are you sure you can't help?'

She wipes her mouth with her sleeve. 'I told you. I don't have a key. My husband took it with him.'

I pause and take a breath. I deliberately look at her front door, then back at her. 'So you can't get back into your own house.'

'Of course I can.' She frowns at me as though I'm stupid. 'I don't have a key for the *back* door. We only have the one.'

'Don't you trust me?'

She folds her arms, exasperated now. 'How many times do I have to tell you? I don't have a key.' She laughs and shakes her head.

'Thanks for your help,' I say. 'Have a nice day.'

I head back down the path. Then I walk the length of the street, to the end of the row of houses. The tongue and groove door that provides access to all the gardens is locked, so I ring the bell of the house next to it. Almost immediately, a young black woman in a dressing gown opens up. A red and blue toy motorbike hangs from her hand.

I recognise her immediately as the woman from the zebra crossing. But she doesn't appear to recognise me.

'Hello,' I say. 'Sorry to bother you. I'm Mr Doran's support worker.'

She narrows her eyes. 'Mr Doran?'

'He lives at number fifty-six.'

Her frown deepens. Her eyes are slightly slanted and her dark iris' have a lighter ring around them, which I didn't notice the first time we met. 'I don't know who you mean,' she says. 'Do I have a dangerous neighbour?'

'No. Not at all. He's only a danger to himself. Self-neglect. That kind of thing. I have to get into his garden. He isn't answering the door and I'm worried he might be ill or has had an accident. He's quite vulnerable at the moment. I need to see in through his back windows, just to make sure.'

The woman nods thoughtfully, biting down on her bottom lip. Then it clicks. The sound of my voice has tripped her memory. 'Oh,' she says. 'I thought you looked familiar. You mean him? He lives on my street?'

'Yes,' I say. 'But it doesn't surprise me that you never saw him. He tends to keep himself to himself. He's probably fine, but I just need to make sure, check all the rooms I can't see into from the street. Could you let me into the alleyway so I can get around the back?'

'Sure,' she says. 'Hang on. I'll go and get the key.'

When she returns, she's no longer carrying the motorbike. She steps outside and closes her front door behind her. She pulls the dressing gown protectively around her and reties the belt. Then she leads me to the alley, keys jangling in her hand. She unlocks the door and pushes it open. 'Just pull it behind you again when you've finished,' she says softly. 'Good luck. I hope he's okay.'

*   *   *

It's 10.15 and I've checked out the back of the flat. His bedroom curtains are still closed. Not even the tiniest gap. On the window ledge are more apples. Six cleanly cut halves laid out in a neat row, the flesh brown but not yet shrivelled, the pips removed. I peer through the kitchen window for the third or fourth time. Definitely no sign of him, or, for that matter, that he's ever been there. Cleanly wiped worktops. No cups out. No cutlery. A neatly folded jay cloth hangs over the spout of the tap. The hall is dim, but I can just about see the post on the carpet. Two brown envelopes, one white.

I walk around to the gap between the houses and press my face against the frosted bathroom window. I can make out virtually nothing, only vague shapes and colours. Set against the buff wall, the foggy edges of the tall pine cupboard. The bath's blurry blue handrail. The soft edge of the door. He could be lying there, only a few feet away from me and I'd never know.

I sit down on an upturned milk crate to think. Sun has filled the back three quarters of the garden. The spider-like shadow of a potted palm dances on a cracked flagstone.

I decide to go back to the woman's house, and when she opens up this time she looks completely different. She's now wearing a tight, cream woollen dress and has applied brown/ gold eye shadow. Her hair, no longer straight, has been transformed into a shiny mass of tight curls. She smells of Palmer's Cocoa Butter and soap.

'No luck,' I tell her, trying hard not to keep glancing at where the dress grips the curve of her waist. 'I can't see in through two of the windows. I think I should maybe call the police but my battery is about to die. Could I use your landline?'

She studies my hair as though it might reveal something deeper about my character. Then she invites me in. 'I'm in a bit of a hurry,' she says over her shoulder as I follow her down the hall, 'otherwise I'd like to be of more help.' Her hips create gentle folds in the wool as she walks. Her head is bent slightly over to the right, both her hands busy fastening an earring. 'It's there,' she says, nodding at the phone as she passes it. She slinks into the kitchen and turns off the radio.

I get a male operator, and as I give my details — my name, Pete's surname and address, details about Open Door — and wondering if the police computer has already made the connection (possible suicide/ suspected arsonist — same address) I pick up a pen and sketch flames on a Post-it pad next to the phone. Then I scribble over them — horizontal lines, verticals, diagonals, loops and spirals — then decide it's probably best to tear the sheet off, so I do, the heel of my

100

hand pinning the pad in place. My scribbles have imprinted on the sheet below, so that one comes off too. Then two more. And another, just to be on the safe side. I crumple the sheets in my hand and slip them into my pocket. The woman, now reading the label on a bottle of pills, hasn't, it seems, witnessed any of this. Humming softly to herself, she places the bottle on the worktop and dusts off her hands.

They will send someone round. Soon. I ask how long 'soon' is and am told that they can never really say. A rough estimate? Twenty five to thirty minutes, probably less. Which I explain is too long. He could be dying in there, in need of oxygen, blood, a jump-start to his heart. I look through to the kitchen again. The woman, now wearing a brown leather waistcoat, is standing in front of her chrome cooker, her hip against the dials. She smiles at me, takes a sip from the orange mug she's holding, then pours the rest into the sink.

I ask the operator if it would be okay to break a window. He tells me that it would because having notified them of my intent I now have what's known as 'power of entry'. He asks if I'd like them to send a car round anyway. I tell him that it isn't necessary. They'll keep a record of my details. If I change my mind I should call back.

'I'll do that,' I say. 'Thanks.' I replace the receiver and look towards the woman. She raises her eyebrows. 'All okay?'

I nod and thank her.

'It's fine.' She picks up a tea towel, folds it, places it on the work surface and gives it a friendly pat. Then she walks towards me, brushing something from her upper arm — fluff, or maybe crumbs — with the back of her other hand. Out of the kitchen, into the hall, another smile as she passes by me, very close, her scent almost edible, like chocolate. I follow her, staring at her V-shaped back, imagining how, compared to the dry boniness of Sarah's, it would feel against my chest. Halfway down the hall I stop in front of a framed child's painting of a purple dog. 'Boy or girl?' I ask.

'Boy.' She opens the front door. 'He's very creative.'

'Fantastic. I love the ears. I don't have kids myself. I don't know if we could afford them.'

The woman grins knowingly. 'Things work themselves out. Money turns up.' She comes and stands next to me and looks at the picture fondly. In profile she's even more beautiful. A smooth muscle, like a dark bulrush, grows from her collarbone to her ear. Her nose is turned up in a perfect curve.

'He's the best and most challenging thing that ever happened to me,' she says. 'It's hard at times, especially on your own, but I wouldn't give him up for the world.'

Which makes me wonder, as I head back down the passage towards Pete's garden, how it must feel to know your parents did just that. Both of them. A unanimous decision. What kind of people would do that to a child?

I begin my search for a suitably heavy object. Eventually I find a half-brick, and when I weigh it in my hand it feels good. I waste no time. I walk straight over to the bedroom window and toss it through.

The smash is fairly unspectacular. No flying shards of glass. No splinters in eyes. No cuts to the face, arms, hands. Two large triangular sheets fall outwards and shatter on the concrete. A half-hearted round of dog barks from a neighbouring garden follows.

I stand there for a while expecting, any minute, to hear a police siren or hurried, skidding footsteps down the passage. Nothing, despite the Neighbourhood Watch Area signs out front. I pluck the remaining loose fragments of glass from the frame. Then prepared for the worst, I open the curtains.

He isn't in there. But what is catches me completely off-guard.

I climb through, and as soon as my head is

inside, I'm struck by how cold the room feels. Two smells compete: mould and gloss paint. He's been busy in here. So this is what the padlock was about.

I step down from the bed onto the wooden floor, which has been painted white.

Map-like drawings are taped to the wall where the door is. On the bedside table is the remainder of the shepherds pie, next to it a fake plastic Yucca plant (also painted white). On the wall, in the shadows cast by its leaves, it says: BLIND BEND. 20th SEPTEMBER 1983.

It doesn't take a genius to work out that the drawings are of the stretch of road where his mother died. There are thirty of them — one for each year that has passed — all in marker pen and pencil on A4 paper.

Two parallel horizontal lines curve upwards, halfway along the paper forming a 90° bend. The lines are not fluid. There's no suggestion of a confidently sweeping pen. These are lines that have been drawn slowly with an uncertain shaking hand. Spots and scratched marks dot the outer edges of the lines (gravel or maybe grass), bringing to mind Beano characters, hairy legs in short pants.

There's something biological about the drawings. They almost have the appearance of medical diagrams. In the top left hand corner of most of them are jagged Ms and Ns that look more like heartbeats on an ECG monitor than the mountains they're obviously supposed to represent. A large circle filled with wavy lines is surrounded by a scribbled path.

Each drawing, though, is slightly different. There are variations — a sign that he's had to trawl his frazzled memory banks for the truth. The angle at which the main road curves is sometimes more than 90°, sometimes less. Two drawings have none of the jagged mountain lines in them at all, and in one there's a hole where he's scribbled frantically. The lake circle varies in shape and size, and the scribbled path doesn't always circle it; sometimes it's straight and runs vertically down the right hand side of the paper.

The two vehicles (black rectangles) have been added — one longer and wider than the other. Blurring suggests they've been repeatedly erased and redrawn, giving them a sense of movement. He's struggled with relative positioning, tried different permutations. Sometimes the rectangles are six inches apart, sometimes closer — five, four, three, half an inch, a quarter. In one instance they touch; in another they blur together to form what looks like a jackknifed lorry.

Next to the window is a small painting of

an apple, similar in style to the potatoes he used to churn out at Lady Gomm — dark background, glowing gradations of green and red. On the other side of the window is a tall thin painting on paper (roughly 6 feet high by 6 inches wide) of what looks like a computer generated, emaciated cactus, the stem pixelated in greens and pinks. On closer inspection I discover the pixels are actually miniature floor plans of rooms. Some are labelled in tiny writing — *Living room; Bathroom; Iris' living room; Dining room; Pat's balcony; Pool room in Commercial; John's parent's terrace* — and the lines indicating door-opening directions act as the cactus' needles.

Suddenly something disturbing catches my eye near the bottom of the cactus. A floor plan with an address written inside it — 38 Apple Blossom Terrace. It's an address I know well. It's my dad's address. A marker pen circle has been drawn around it, and an arrow veers away towards a collage of photographs — some from Pete's childhood, some of cars, one of a dog, several of Iris.

My stomach takes a roll and the feeling I had in Dali's house becomes a reality. Smack-bang in the centre of the collage is a gloomy snap of 38 Apple Blossom Terrace taken from across the road. Creepier still is that I can tell exactly when it was taken. Sarah's car is on the driveway. And in the living room window is a Christmas tree. My mother's bedroom light is on. It's likely that I'm up there with her, massaging her feet.

Suddenly I hear the front door click open followed by Iris' throaty laugh. 'I know,' she rasps, 'that's what I thought.'

I try the door, hoping to God that the padlock isn't snapped closed on the other side. Luckily it isn't, and I step into the hall.

The two of them stop dead in their tracks, blue and white striped plastic bags hanging from their hands. The three of us look at each other for a moment. Pete looks especially nervous.

'Nice morning?' I say.

He frowns. 'How did *you* get in?'

'How do you think I got in? I broke a window.'

'Which one?'

'Three guesses.'

His eyes widen. 'Why?'

'Why? I also called the police. But then I imagine they were already intending to pay you a visit anyway.'

Iris sheepishly dips her head and disappears into the living room. Pete follows her. I walk to the doorway. 'Did you forget I was coming?'

He drops the plastic bags next to the coffee

table and backs away from them. 'No.'
Slumping into his armchair, he sighs like a
sulky teenager.

'Don't sigh at me,' I say. 'If anyone should
be sighing it's me.'

'Here we go,' Iris says. 'No wonder he's not
well. You nagging him the whole time.'

Iris has placed herself in the centre of the
sofa and is flicking through a magazine. She's
a big woman — maybe twice Pete's width and
weight. She's wearing a light brown fake-fur
coat, a string of pearls, and beige nylon trousers. Her face is flushed, her eyelids metallic
light blue, and since I last saw her she's had
blonde streaks introduced to her short, mousy
hair. There's a scratch on her cheek and some
fairly dark bruising near her temple. The con-
cealer she's used is not even close to the right
tone for her skin.

'You shouldn't have taken him out when he
knew I was coming,' I tell her.

She lets the magazine flop into her lap. 'I
didn't *take* him anywhere. What do you think
he is, a dog? Anyway, he said you weren't
cooking today.' She turns to Pete. 'Isn't that
right, love?'

Pete smiles timidly.

She picks up the magazine again. 'He doesn't
need day centres. He's got people. Haven't
you?'

.Nodding, but clearly with some uncertainty, Pete takes a last, painful looking drag on his cigarette, then leans forward to stub it out in the ashtray. 'I think you'd better go,' he tells Iris. 'I might see you at the club tonight.'

Iris shrugs. 'You two rattling around in here every morning. It's not right.' She gathers her things together and heaves herself to standing.

I step aside to let her into the hall and I follow her as she heads for the front door.

'I used to think you were nice,' she says over her shoulder. 'You think you know what's best for him but you haven't got a clue.' She opens the front door, steps outside and turns to face me. 'Nobody cares about him as much as I do. No-one. You ask him.'

'I hear you're getting married.'

'You hear right.'

'Good luck with that.'

She shakes her head and sighs. 'You think you're so bloody clever.'

'I mean it,' I say sincerely.

'John's a good man.'

'Who said he wasn't?'

'He is.'

I glance at the crusty scratch on her face. 'As long as you think so. That's the main thing.'

She flicks her head at the bay window. '*He's* going to be best man.'

'That's decent of him,' I say. 'If he hasn't been banged up for arson by then, I'm sure he'll do a great job.'

'He wouldn't have meant any real harm — if it *was* him. He likes John. And he likes his parents too.'

'Whatever you say.'

'Ask him. He'd do anything for me.'

I nod. 'I believe *that.*'

At this she closes her eyes briefly. Then she turns and walks away. I expect her to stop at the gate and deliver a final, winning one-liner. But she doesn't, she surprises me by not even looking back.

I close the door and head back to the living room, where I find Pete standing in the bay window, not looking through it forlornly, not charting Iris' progress as she heads off down the street, but studying the fingers of his right hand in the light streaming in, a sinister grin playing across his face. 'Look at this,' he says, gesturing me over with a flick of his head.

I go and stand beside him and he presents both hands. The whorls of his fingerprints are black, defined. He looks at me. 'Don't you think they look like contour lines on an Ordinance Survey map?'

'Okay,' I say. 'This has gone far enough.'

He feigns confusion. 'I don't know what you mean.'

'My paintings. You've never seen them and yet you'd say something like that?'

'What? You paint? You paint fingerprints?'

'When did she show them to you? It was obviously her.'

'Who?'

'Please don't treat me like an idiot Pete. When did she show you my slides?'

'She didn't. I looked at them online.'

'But I never even told you I was an artist.'

'I had a vision — '

'And please don't start with that again.'

'You take me to galleries, you lend me books about painters, and you don't expect me to put two and two together?'

'Fine. Don't worry about it. I'll find out from her. What *is* that on your hands anyway?'

'Oil. Or maybe soot.'

'From what?'

'I can't remember.' He chuckles. 'Something or other.'

'Pete, we need to talk.'

He turns his hands over and looks at his nails. 'The letters or the photograph?'

'I'm not interested in the letters. The first one was just plain stupid, knowing who I'd think it was. As for the second, yes, very impressive, thanks, but I'm really not much into poetry. The photograph of my dad's house 250 miles away, though, you definitely need to tell me about.'

'She died,' he says. 'And now we're both motherless. You should have told me when we met. I'd have understood. I know how it feels.'

My mind suddenly feels like it's being bent out of shape. Six weeks before I even meet him, Pete's outside my parents house taking photographs. A few days later my mother dies. A week after that Pete tries to kill himself. The chronology makes no sense. 'Sarah told you she was ill, didn't she? She told you about meeting me, and then she blabbed that my mother was ill.'

He shakes his head.

'Then how did you know? And what were you doing up there?'

'I wanted to find out about you. It's not such a big deal. How was I to know you'd end up being my support worker? I wasn't even planning to be alive.'

'What could you possibly find out about me by making a 500 mile round trip just to sit outside my dying mother's house and take snaps? It would be different if you'd been outside my house, but you weren't, were you? That too. Jesus Christ! I can't believe she told you where we lived. I know she has a lot going on at the moment, but she should know better than that.'

'She didn't. I think I might have looked in your address book.'

'You've got a fucking nerve, going through my bag.'

'You leave it open on the worktop. You're always leaving things out.'

'And what? That's an invitation for you to go rooting through my stuff?'

'I don't understand why you're getting angry and swearing. It wasn't meant to turn out like this. I pictured it all differently.'

'I'm getting angry, Pete, because last night you almost set fire to someone's house. Remember? And in your bedroom I just found a photograph of my dad's house.'

'You have no proof about the fire. And no-one will find any.'

'Yes, I imagine you made sure of that.'

He sighs heavily. 'It isn't easy, is it? Losing your mother.'

'No,' I say. 'Of course it isn't.'

'And time doesn't help, either. Time the great healer. Sorry to be the bearer of bad news, but it hasn't been like that for me. I'm sure you can probably see that. You tick along for years and then it all just hits you one day for no reason. Ten years. Twenty. Thirty. Bang.' His face darkens suddenly. Tears well in his eyes but he quickly blinks them away. 'I want to build a model,' he says. 'Like Hopper

113

did, but with trees and mountains and a lake and a road. We can do it together. You could help me.'

I shake my head. 'I really don't think I can help you with anything, Pete. Not anymore.'

10

It's 5.30 in the morning and a text has just come through from Sarah. Despite countless attempts to contact her, it's the first I've heard from her in seven hours: *Sorry bad signal here only just got your messages. Can't talk on the mway back around 6.30 meet me at the lido for the early-bird swim?*

It's just approaching a quarter past when I enter the park at the South Gate. I head towards the North Gate where Pete lives. All the way there I'm thinking that my legs will take me past the lido, out of the gate, across the infamous zebra crossing and then first right into Warmington Rd. What will he be doing? Sleeping? Scribbling away on the bedroom walls? Building a dirty bomb?

Alone so early in the park, only the birds for company, I suddenly feel vulnerable and reluctant to ever set foot through his front door again. Despite Sarah's words of reassurance, I really could be in danger there. What could be more potentially dangerous than a suicidal man with a mental health problem? A man like that has nothing to lose.

As I pass the tennis courts I glance at the

surrounding bush and picture him hiding in the one opposite my parents house. Only a few days before Christmas and that's what he was up to. Tragic. Was he actually hiding down there as my mother was telling me about the crash? What if I'd got up afterwards, to close the curtains, looked out of the window and spotted the glowing tip of his cigarette? What if my dad had seen him on his way out to the pub? What if he'd marched over there, taken him by the scruff of the neck, dragged him inside and thrown him face down on the living room carpet? 'David, this man claims he knows Sarah.'

⋆ ⋆ ⋆

Sarah is sitting poolside when I arrive at the lido, just up from two children who are trying to climb aboard an inflatable crocodile. 'It would be easier if you held it,' she shouts to the boy. 'Then your sister can get on first.' The boy grabs the plastic handles attached to the crocodile's head and his sister slides up its back. The two of them paddle away, laughing and splashing, the crocodile bent in half.

I pull up a chair and start by being polite. 'How was the journey back?'

'Fine. Clear.'

'What time did you leave Devon?'

'4.30ish.'

'Aren't you exhausted?'

'A bit.'

'I brought some of your things. I couldn't find your shampoo.'

'I had it with me. Thanks though.'

I place the carrier bag on her knee and she looks at me expectantly.

'Let's swim,' I say. 'Then we can talk.'

'I don't need to talk,' she says.

'I didn't mean you. I meant me.'

'Okay,' she shrugs. 'Fine.'

I change into my shorts and head for the shallow end. The water is cold, but not as cold as I expected. I float around for a while. Then I swim a few clumsy widths. It feels odd that the water I'm splashing about in is the same water sliding off Sarah's body as she powers up and down the fast lane. She has a pretty good stroke, strong and smooth. But she makes swimming look more like a punishment than a pleasure.

Twenty minutes later, showered and trying not to dwell on how shockingly thin she looked in her swimming costume, I sit waiting for her to change back into her clothes. As usual she takes her time, washing her hair and putting on creams and lotions. I go to the kiosk and order toast for the two of us, plus two teas. Leaning against a plastic breakfast table I watch the sunlight play on the water.

Petrol. A match. Whoosh!

A whole day has now gone by and Pete still hasn't been questioned. If he is, how will he slip up? What will it be that puts him in the frame? No plastic fuel container was found by the pool. It could be anywhere. He could have buried it, burned it, tossed it into a bush. Will it be Iris who eventually coaxes out the truth? Or might he just casually toss it into the conversation one morning as we cook?

Sarah emerges from the changing rooms. I pay for the order and head back towards my table, the paper plate of toast balanced precariously on top of the two teas. She's draping her swimming costume over the back of a chair and spreading her towel out on the floor next to it. Sighing contentedly, she flops to sitting.

'How was it?'

'Hard work,' she says.

'How many lengths?'

'Ten.'

'I don't know how you do it. I'd probably need a rest between each one. Here, I got you some toast and tea.'

'I've been counting my strokes over the last couple of weeks,' she says, taking the paper plate. 'Sixty per length. I keep thinking it will get less, but it doesn't. Someone once told me that the ideal leg kick is with your knees brushing together. You're also supposed to rock in the water, really rock from side to side, and the most important part of the arms is the last push backwards, the final scoop. It's a lot to remember. A lot to concentrate on at once.'

I nod, noticing how slowly she's eating the toast, how she's tearing off small pieces and chewing them tentatively. I finish both my slices before she's eaten half of her first. She looks up as I'm rinsing down the last mouthful. 'You don't need to watch me like that.'

'Sorry,' I say.

She smiles her irritated smile.

'Sarah, I think I should probably call the police.'

'Why. So they can section him again?'

'It might be the best thing for him.'

'You mean the best thing for you?'

'Fucking hell. You make it sound as though I'm being irrational for wanting to feel safe.'

'He doesn't need to be sectioned, David. And you aren't qualified to make that call anyway. You've only been working your job for four months — part time, I might add. Just because I pulled strings to get you a job,

119

and you've read a few books and been on some training courses, it doesn't mean you're suddenly a psychiatrist. I've been in the field for four years. I know what I'm talking about.'

'Well then you'd think you'd know better than to tell clients where we live.'

'I didn't.'

'You did. I know you did. The letters. They were from him. But that's done now. It doesn't matter and I'm not going to sit here and argue with you about it. The thing is, I found something in his bedroom yesterday, something pretty frightening.'

'What?'

'You probably already know.'

'I don't. Otherwise I wouldn't be asking.'

'At the hospice, the thing he was worried you might have told me — '

'That again.'

'Yes. That again.'

'I can't.'

'You can't what?'

'I can't tell you.'

'So there is something.'

'Yes. I'm sorry. But when I give my word to someone I keep it.'

I get to my feet, furious now. 'I can't believe you can lie so convincingly. Jesus! You made me feel like I was stupid for even asking you about it.'

'Look, David. He's of no threat to you. I've known him longer than you have. That's not what this is all about.'

'All about? What is it *all about?*'

'I can't tell you.'

'I'm his key worker, Sarah. And you don't even work for Open Door anymore. A mentally ill man travels 250 miles to take a photograph of my parent's house, while my mother's dying — before I even meet him. There you go. That's what I fucking found in his room. What about that! A mentally ill man who, it turns out, likes to set fire to things by pouring petrol on them. Does any of that sound okay to you?'

Sarah glances around, concerned that I'm raising my voice and spoiling the relaxing atmosphere for everyone. Calmly, she gestures for me to sit down again, which I do. 'It's nothing like you think,' she says. 'He'd never hurt you. You or anyone.'

'I don't think you have a clue — '

She holds up her hand and cuts me off. 'David, do you know what? I don't want to discuss this here. I made a promise to myself while I was away that I wouldn't do this kind of thing again, like we did at the hospice. I don't want to be someone who's known for always arguing in public places. I hate that kind of thing. It's shabby.'

'Well that's fucking wonderful for you,' I say. 'Because, you know, I'd hate to think I was stunting your spiritual growth.'

'You're raising your voice again.'

'I wouldn't need to if you'd tell me the truth.'

'I can't.'

'Then I need to phone Phil and tell him I won't be going around there anymore. I don't feel safe. I — '

'Okay,' she says. 'Okay. Have it your way. He used to have a thing about me. Satisfied?'

'A thing?'

'Yes. A thing. He got upset when I started going out with someone. That's why he stopped coming to Lady Gomm.'

'Sarah, I already know all this. I worked it out for myself. I'm not fucking stupid.'

'You asked me to tell you, and there it is.'

'And on top of telling him you were going out with someone, you thought it might be a good idea to tell him who the someone was, and while you were at it you thought you'd throw in his parents fucking address as well?'

'Okay, I might have let it slip that we were going up there regularly, because of your mum. I might have told him the fucking address. Happy?' She throws her paper plate down on the table and it knocks over her tea but she doesn't seem to care. 'Don't you think I already have enough going on as it is? Do you think I really need *this* on top of everything else? I thought you of all people would understand that. I don't know why I bothered. I should never have got involved in the first place.'

'Involved? Involved with what?'

She holds up a hand again. 'No. That really *is* it now. No more. I mean it. You're just going to have to trust me.' She stuffs her wash bag into her rucksack and stands. 'So. What are you doing today?' she says casually, as though we've just been discussing the weather.

'I don't know. I might go to the studio, but I think I'll stay here for a while first.'

'Will you be back late?'

'I've no idea.'

'Well let me know what your plans are. I don't have any.'

'I'm not finished with this, Sarah. Just so you know.'

'You'll have to be. Because I am.'

I watch her walk around the edge of the pool, her orange corduroy skirt twitching stiffly with each brisk step. She turns and waves. Then she passes through the turnstile.

★ ★ ★

Twenty minutes later I'm outside Pete's. There's a note taped to the front door. The handwriting is slightly different to the hand-writing in the letters, and the thought of him deliberately disguising it for my benefit doesn't seem sinister, just pathetic: *Gone to Model-Zone up in Holborn. See you tomorrow. Don't break any windows. No new photographs to see.*

I head over to the studio where I potter around for a few hours, listening to the radio, working in my sketchpad, drinking tea, eating Jaffa Cakes. Around lunchtime, as I'm flicking through a book about colour theory, Sarah calls to say that Clare's had a terrible morning and could use some company.

★　★　★

When I arrive home she's ready to go, jacket on, rucksack balanced on her knee, eyes puffy. Any further questions I might have about Pete are shelved.

In the car I lean across the seat and lift the lock button. Sarah gets in and slams the door. 'I need my life back,' she says. 'I feel like I'm losing my fucking mind.'

'You're doing okay,' I tell her.

She sighs heavily. 'I really thought I *was* doing okay today. But I can already feel myself tensing up.' She turns and stares out of the window. 'I wish it was somewhere else we were going. Somewhere nice.'

I nod. 'I don't feel up to it today either, if I'm honest.'

'You don't have to come. I didn't tell her we were both coming.' She bends forwards and touches her forehead onto her knees. She stays like this for a while before sitting up again.

'By the way, I forgot to mention. Your mum phoned while you were in Devon.'

'Why?'

'She wondered if you could do some of the evening shifts next week.'

'When next week?'

'Tuesday. Thursday.'

'Tuesday *and* Thursday or Tuesday *or* Thursday?'

'I can't remember. It was early. I wasn't completely awake.'

'Put your seat belt on,' she says.

I do, then pull away.

★   ★   ★

Half an hour later we turn into the hospice car park. The tyres crunch on the gravel and I steer over to the left, resisting the urge to do an inappropriate but spectacular handbrake turn. Sensibly, gently, I press the brake and we come to a slow stop under a tree. The light twinkling through the leaves and branches raises my spirits momentarily.

But heading up the stairs, Sarah a full flight in front of me, the photograph of 38 Apple Blossom Terrace comes back to me with Sarah's reassuring words as accompaniment: 'He'd never hurt anyone.'

And then I'm on Clare's floor. Focus. She will need our full attention.

She's working on the handmade wooden jigsaw of two owls on a branch when we enter her room. I bought it for her three weeks ago. It wasn't cheap. Each piece is a different but themed shape — a tree, an eagle, a sparrow, a pelican. A sticker on the box said the age range was ten years to adult, but I peeled it off before giving it to her.

I lean over and kiss her cheek, shocked by how pale she looks. The semi-transparent skin of her temples looks like greaseproof paper that's been in the oven. She smells bitter. Antiseptic. Like a cat back from the vets.

'How are you doing?' Sarah asks her. She leans over the bed to hug her.

'Terrible. My back's awful today.'

The two of them hold each other for a while, and when Sarah eventually lets go and sits down on the bed, Clare flinches. 'Can you get up a minute,' she says, her voice thin and shaky. 'My tube's trapped.'

Sarah stands up quickly. 'Sorry.'

126

'It's fine, you can sit down again now.'

'How are your legs?' I ask hopefully.

'Huge,' she says. 'Look.' She smoothes the bedclothes over her left thigh. It's almost the size of both mine together. She looks at Sarah. 'Happy now? You've stormed ahead.'

'Does the massage help?' Sarah asks awkwardly.

'It makes me *feel* a little better, I suppose.'

'Shall I make some tea?' I ask.

Clare shakes her head. 'I've just had one.'

'I'd like one,' Sarah says. 'Decaf. Is there any soya milk?'

Clare hiccups. 'There should be. I think mum brought some yesterday.'

Squatting, I open the fridge door, and the unpleasant smell of fermenting fruit wafts out. On the middle shelf are two Ski yoghurts, their foil tops swollen and taut. I press one with my finger. Then I take out the milk and carton of Alpro.

'Okay,' I say. 'Back in a minute.'

The two of them nod.

The first thing I do is go to the disabled bathroom. It smells like it's been recently used but at least I can get a minute to myself in here. Once I've locked the door I flip the toilet seat down and sit on it, feeling suddenly overwhelmed and far more sorry for myself than I probably should in a place like this. My

127

mother was lucky to live out her last days at home.

I stand up and walk over to the sink. I half fill the basin with cold water and splash my face a few times. I dab it dry, take a breath, and brace myself for a long afternoon.

Sarah's holding Clare's hand when I get back with the teas. The two of them have been crying. I pretend not to notice.

'If ever I get a headache, tea always sorts it out,' I say cheerfully.

'That's because you're addicted to tannin,' Clare says. 'It's not that the tea takes away your headache, the tea's the reason you have the headache in the first place.'

'Maybe,' I say.

'Not maybe,' she says. 'That's a fact.'

'Shall I help with the jigsaw?'

'It's up to you. You bought it.'

'We can all do it together.'

'You two can,' Sarah says, getting to her feet. 'I'm going to go and pick up some things from around the corner.'

'What about your tea?'

'It's okay,' she says. 'You drink both. I won't be long. See you in a minute.' She opens the door and she's gone.

I sit down and begin gathering grey pieces together, Clare green ones. I slot a stork-shaped piece in place and search for the one that fits it. I'm working on the left hand owl's chest. It's almost finished. Four more pieces. Maybe five. 'This bit's almost impossible,' I say. 'The whole area's just greys and browns.'

'Stick with it,' she says. 'You have to be patient.'

I find an eagle-shaped piece and slot it in place below the right hand owl's beak.

Clare nods, teacher-like. 'See,' she says without looking up. 'Patience.' She pauses, frowning. 'How old do you think this photograph is?'

'I've no idea. It doesn't look very old.'

'They're probably both dead now. How long do owls live?'

'For quite a long time, I think.'

She scowls playfully. 'You have no idea. Have you?'

'Not really,' I say. 'But I think they do.'

She shakes her head. 'It's ridiculous, when you think about it. Pointless. We're doing this, putting all this work in, and I know someone will take it apart and box it up in seconds after I'm gone.' She tries to take a deep breath but can't. 'All that Buddhist nonsense about transience and change is all very well when you have a future. Give me the myth of permanence any day.'

'I agree. Ignorance is bliss.'

'Don't speak in clichés,' she says. 'You're

supposed to be an artist.'

'I just make paintings. I never said I was Kant.'

'Facking Kant maybe.'

This is without doubt the funniest thing Clare has ever said in my presence, and the two of us laugh for much longer than we need to, with a certain kind of desperation.

'I need my drink,' she eventually says.

I pass her Ribena over and watch her prominent Adam's apple bob up and down as she drains the glass. She wipes her mouth with the back of her hand and picks up three brown out-of-focus, tree-shaped pieces. 'You carry on with the fence,' she says. 'Here, these are all parts of it.'

'I once read this book,' I say. '*Dibs in search of Self*. It's by a child therapist. Dibs was the name of a boy she worked with.'

'Dibs?'

'I don't know if it was his real name.'

'No wonder he needed a therapist. Did you know Sarah had to see a therapist when she was a teenager?'

I shake my head.

'No, of course you didn't. She doesn't give much away. *I* hardly know her at all and I'm her big sister. Don't you want to know why?'

'I think I can probably guess. Eating disorder?'

'You've had enough,' she says. 'You've given up on her, haven't you? I can hear it in your voice. She never gets anyone to stay with her for very long.'

'We're not getting on at the moment. We're both exhausted.'

'Because of me?'

'No,' I lie. 'Of course not.'

'Don't worry,' she says. 'It will all be over soon.'

An awkward moment passes, and when it feels as though it's been sufficiently honoured, I steer us back toward my anecdote. 'There's a passage in the book where Dibs is playing with a cardboard fence,' I say. 'He picks up one of the negative shapes, the bits of cardboard that have been punched out from in-between the fence posts, and he says to the therapist, 'This is a piece of nowhere. This is what nowhere looks like'.'

Clare coughs a glob of phlegm into a tissue and then wipes her mouth. 'Great,' she says. 'Thanks for that. At least I'll now be able to recognise it when I get there.'

★ ★ ★

For most of the journey home, Sarah and I hardly say a word. We are soiled, defeated, three points short of the relegation zone.

Cancer is lathered up and singing in the showers.

Sarah drives and I stare out of the passenger side window thinking about my work. It's a welcome distraction.

An idea is forming. A series of paintings with clichés as titles.

Clichés are due a makeover (though to be honest I've never understood what everyone has against them in the first place). Clichés are perfect, they can't be improved upon; that's why people hate them. I make a mental note of three good ones:

The darkest hour is just before the dawn.

Take the rough with the smooth.

Long time, no see.

★ ★ ★

It's 8 p.m. and I've just received a phone call from a woman, a stranger, informing me that Pete is in St Thomas' hospital after throwing himself from the back of a Routemaster bus.

When it rains it pours.

Minor head injuries. Clean break to his ankle. Ligaments torn from the bone. The woman knows all this because she followed the ambulance to A&E so that Pete wouldn't have to be there on his own.

She said she'd never seen anything quite

like it. Why would anyone want to do such a thing? It happened up in Holborn, outside a model shop.

She'd been driving behind the bus for a while and Pete had waved at her several times. But then the waving stopped and he began to make strange movements with his hands, movements she described as similar to those a magician might make when casting a spell. His grin changed, and the woman said she thought to herself, 'something is going to happen to that man, something bad'. Her estimate was that they were travelling at 25 to 30 miles an hour when he shuffled forwards looking down at his feet, as though assessing the suitability of his footwear for the jump and subsequent landing ahead. When he looked up there were tears in his eyes, and at that point the woman thought about beeping her horn in the hope that it would shock him back to his senses. She didn't, though, she just watched helplessly, her hands frozen to the wheel, as he mouthed something, closed his eyes, bit his lip, and stepped off the platform.

He almost managed to stay upright, she said, seemed to give it his best shot. And if his expression was anything to go by he'd almost certainly had second thoughts as soon as he'd let go of the pole. It was no use, though, too late, he didn't appear to have the leg-strength to recover. He landed, skipped backwards a few steps, hopped, changed feet. But then his legs buckled under him and he went down heavily on his side. The woman pulled over, and by the time she'd made her way to him, a small gathering of people had formed. Miraculously, he was sitting up, his face pale green, his lower leg bent in half, something very bone-like protruding from a hole in his jeans. He smiled sheepishly when he saw the woman. Then he retched and was sick over himself. She described a large, fresh white cut on his forehead that was bleeding into his eye.

It's been stitched by the time I get to the hospital and looks nasty/impressive. They've given him a bed for the night so they can keep an eye on him. He's awake, and despite his best efforts not to show it, I can tell he's pleased to see me.

'So,' I say. 'I think it might be time to give up on the bus thing. It doesn't seem to be working for you.'

'I don't know what you mean.'

'I think you probably do.'

'I fainted. It was an accident.'

I pull a chair up to his bed. 'The woman said it looked like you stepped off the platform on purpose. Why would you do that?'

'I don't think I did it on purpose.'

'You don't think.'

'No. I saw the model shop, realised I'd missed the stop, and panicked.'

'And then fainted.'

'Yes.'

'The woman described it differently.'

He shrugs. 'I don't know. I can't remember. But it doesn't matter anyway because I'm okay. Will you get the things we need? The shop's called ModelZone. You can't miss it. It's huge. You could go in the morning. I imagine I'll still be in here. If they have anything else interesting, other than the car and the van, get that too.'

'I'm not even sure I can carry on seeing you, Pete, let alone go to a model shop. I need to speak to Phil about everything that's happened recently. I can't not tell my manager.'

He sits up in bed. 'No, please don't do that. I missed a few pills and lied that I'd taken them. I know I've been acting strange lately. But it won't happen again. Honestly.'

'I'm not talking about lately. I'm not even interested in whether or not it was you who lit the fire. I mean the photograph. I know you were off your medication back then, and I know you were in a bad way, but I have to put my dad first. He's the only family I have now.

If you did anything like that again — whether you knew what you were doing or not — and anything happened to him, I'd regret it for the rest of my life.'

'Nothing will happen to him, I promise. It wasn't about him. It was about you. Look at me, anyway. I can't even walk now.'

I look at his bright red cast. One of the nurses has already signed it and added an X. 'Put yourself in my position,' I say. 'Would you trust the promises of someone with a track record like yours? I don't mean that disrespectfully. I'm just being realistic.'

'I was always honest with you about how bad things can get with me. I never tried to pretend I was normal. I wouldn't have given you the handout if I'd wanted to do that.'

'Yes,' I say, 'and I admire that. But still, would you?'

'No. Probably not.'

'So you see my position.'

'I'd never hurt anyone. I know the stories of mentally ill people stabbing total strangers in the street. You know me though. You know I'm not dangerous.'

'I thought I did.'

'You do. Four months is long enough to get to know someone. I only went up there because I wanted to see the type of person she'd got involved with. I cared about her, she'd done a lot for me, and I just wanted to make sure she knew what she was getting into.'

'Very noble. But believe me, Pete, Sarah is more than capable of taking care of herself.'

'I know. I can see that now. But I couldn't see anything back then. I didn't even want to live anymore.'

I feel myself softening. The anger is slowly leaving me. I look at him and he does cut a pretty pathetic figure. If I abandon him now, who will step in? Iris? 'I need to think about all of this,' I say. 'I need to sleep on it. And I won't tell Phil anything until I've done that. I give you my word.'

He relaxes visibly. 'Thanks.'

'I have to go now. I'm shattered.'

'Will you do me a favour? When you *have* slept on it, and if you do decide not to tell Phil, could you go to the flat and take down the drawings and everything else. If anyone sees them while I'm in here, well, I just don't want them to.'

'Give me your keys and I'll see what I can do.'

He reaches into his drawer and hands them to me.

'How many of the drawings are there, in total? Just the ones I saw?'

'No. About a hundred and fifty.'

'Wow!'

'There's nothing *wow* about it. Have you only done a handful of paintings?'

'No.'

'Why not?'

'Because no painting is ever a complete success, and you hope the next one will be, but it never is, so you do another one.'

'Exactly. There you go. The only difference is, I'm not interested in success.'

'They're fascinating.'

'They're not meant to be.'

'I know. That's probably why they are. Where is the place, anyway?'

'I don't know. I know what it looks like but can't remember where it is.'

At this point I think of something. One common feature of the drawings was that the actual drawn area was small in relation to the size of the paper. Teachers tell children off for this kind of thing all the time — use all of the paper; that's what it's there for — but in Pete's case I'm hoping it was deliberate. Early European maps left unchartered areas a mysterious blank. Medieval maps filled the areas beyond known borders with monsters and dragons. Eventually, knowledge grew outwards, bloomed like a stain, until nothing unknown remained, and the monsters and dragons were forced off the paper.

'So they're anti maps,' I say. 'Maps of nowhere.'

'I don't know what they are. They're just something I needed to do for myself.'

'I like the painting of the apple.'

'More than the real ones I left for you?'

'Yes. Clever. New York. The Big Apple. Apple Blossom Terrace. Very good. The one you left at John's parents' pond was maybe not such a good idea.'

'Oh well. A bit late now.'

'The cactus piece is good too.'

'All the rooms I've ever been in.'

'And it grows upwards, in the order you were in the rooms. Right?'

'Right.'

'But my parent's address was on there. You were never in the house.'

'No, not the house. The drive and the flagged bit around the back.'

'You were on the drive and the bit around the back?'

'Only briefly.'

'When?'

'Just before I left. I looked through the glass doors.'

'And did you see anything?'

'No. No-one was around.'

I get to my feet. 'I have to go. I really have to go now.'

'We can make the model in my shed,' he says. 'I already cleared it out.'

* * *

I leave the hospital fairly sure that I'll call Phil first thing and tell him everything. I have a duty to, for everyone's sake — mine, Pete's, my dad's. But oddly enough, by the time I'm halfway home, all sense of menace seems to have passed, and it seems ridiculous suddenly to think that I might be in danger. I remind myself of the following things: Pete is 'tragic' mentally ill, not secure unit material. He isn't a sociopath. He's funny at times, interesting, full of surprises, has no history of violence towards others, and only lit the pond fire because John broke his heart by stealing Iris'. As for Sarah, he must know — must have always known — that he never stood a realistic chance with her. There's no good reason whatsoever why he would want to harm me.

I pull up outside home feeling only empathy for him, and a surprising enthusiasm for the model. When he first suggested it, I cringed — it sounded like something a parent might be talked into after having watched *Art Attack* with their seven year old. If I do continue working with him, it will be

140

something interesting to do together. One thing's for sure, it will beat watching daytime TV.

Carer and Psychiatric Patient Build Crash Reconstruction as Therapy.

We could even end up in *Metro*.

11

It's just before 9 a.m. and I'm outside ModelZone waiting for someone to open up.

The window display is an eclectic mix of small, die-cast cars — *Chitty Chitty Bang Bang*, the red Austin 1100 from *Fawlty Towers*, all three Minis from *The Italian Job* — and trains, planes, boats and action figures.

An old man appears before long and unlocks. I head inside.

The shop is huge and smells of new carpet. On the left, just inside the entrance, I spot a wall full of figure kits and I head over to them. *The Bell Ringer of Notre Dame. King Kong. Godzilla* and *Wolfman*. Some of the box illustrations are pretty impressive. *The Forgotten Prisoner of Gastel Mare*'s skull has fallen sadly to the side, his glow-in-the-dark ribcage bursting out through his rotten, tattered shirt. There's a model *Bates Motel* set against a darkening sky, Norman's mother looking menacingly down from an upstairs window.

I wander between the aisles, peering into the glass display cabinets, absently picking boxes and putting them back again. I used to build models as a child; it's what only children do. Henry the Eighth. The Black Prince. Harley Davidsons. Tanks with real rubber tracks. It's all about prep work. Newspaper down. Paint the parts before snapping them off the sprue. Sailing ships are tricky. Tiny cannons and real cotton rigging.

The shop slowly fills up — a surprising mix of teenagers and office types in suits (young and old). I look around for an assistant and pick the one who opened up — grey beard, experienced looking. As I approach him I notice that his name (Gerry) is embroidered on his breast pocket. He looks up and smiles. 'Yes, sir?'

'I don't know if this is possible,' I say, 'and I can't see one anywhere, but what are the chances of getting a self assembly van? A transit, say.'

'Mmm. I haven't seen one for, ooh, what, ten years?'

'I see.'

Gerry folds his arms and looks down at the carpet. 'No, I don't know of one at all I'm afraid. I mean there might be one in resin, or white metal.'

'I don't know what that means,' I say. 'I'm a bit out of date with all this. I'm building a model with a friend. A scene.'

'What scale?'

'The base will be 8ft × 4ft. We need a car and a Transit. But the only car I've seen so far that would be appropriate is a 1/24 scale Mini.'

'Right. Okay. Well what scale did you *want?*'

'Well, that scale looks about right, I suppose. But it wasn't really a Mini we were after. We were looking for an old Volvo saloon, mid 80s, but I haven't seen one of those either, not even in the small die-cast ones.'

Gerry nods, mulling something over. 'The only one that springs to mind is the racing one from the British Touring Club. But again that was quite a few years ago. You could try St Martin's Accessories in St Martin's Lane. They might have it.'

'Would it be self assembly?'

'I doubt it. Are you sure 1/24 scale is definitely what you want?'

'I think so.'

'Your Transit's going to be a problem.'

'I see.'

'There might be — ' he pauses again. ' — You definitely have to build it yourself. Is that very important?'

'We'd prefer to, if possible.'

'In that case, I'm not sure I can help you. I'm sorry I can't be of more assistance.'

'Thanks,' I say. 'I'll carry on looking.' And I head towards the glass display cabinets to my right.

I spend the next ten to fifteen minutes trying to find an appropriate model car, but without much success. Most are too modern, and in the end I have no option but to settle for the Mini. There are two, both 1/24 scale, same make (Revell) almost identical box. I take them off the shelf and get down on my knees to compare them. I'm confused. One that's white is £9.99, the other, red, is £14.99. Apart from that, the illustrations are identical. Same pavilion. Same grass. Same helmeted racing driver with hands in pockets. Same alice band wearing girl, her hand semi-erotically resting on the Mini's wing.

While no-one's looking I break the Sellotape holding the lids in place with my thumbnail. But even now, both boxes open and side by side, I can still see no difference. Same radiator grill. Same bonnet. Same tyres and chassis. Same silver wing mirrors and wheels. It's only when I examine the transfers that I notice the cheaper model has Japanese number plates. I swap them for the English ones, replace the lids, and put the more expensive model back on the shelf.

The only van I can find is a VW Camper, 1/24 scale. The illustration shows it with orange bodywork and a cream roof, parked on a beach, a laughing man and woman playing frisbee nearby.

I take it down off the shelf.

On the way over to the till I stop to look through the model making accessories rack. Plastic houses. Windmills. Pylons. Signals that change if used in conjunction with the programmable control box. Small see-through bags of different coloured powders — scatter material — the different colours listed on a chart: Foliage green; Foliage brown; Grass; Sandstone; Beach; Tarmac.

I unhook two bags of Tarmac and one of Grass.

Model trees. Different types. But all much too small for 1/24 scale cars. The green, toilet brush pines are the nearest match, but still not quite what we're looking for. Rolls of green and light brown matting. Tiny drystone walls. A footbridge. A packet of sheep. A small grey barn with a broken door.

Gerry is now at the Hornby counter, flicking through a catalogue. I walk over to him. 'One last question,' I say. 'If you were building a model with 1/24 cars, how would you do the trees?'

'Phoo,' he says. 'You're looking at some pretty big trees there.' He places both palms on the glass counter. 'Do you like grapes?'

I nod, slightly confused.

'The stalks,' he says. 'That's what some model makers use for trees or shrubbery. You have to paint them, of course, or treat them with varnish or woodstain, something hardening, otherwise they tend to whither and droop. They look best brown or dark green. You build a trunk from clay and while the clay's still moist you stick the grape stalks in, angled upwards. I'm sure you've looked at trees.'

'Yes,' I say. 'I've looked at trees.'

He smiles. 'As I said, they *are* going to be pretty big objects. If you think that those over there are only 00 gauge, well, yours are going to be huge in comparison.'

'Is that a problem?'

'I suppose it depends how much room you have. Your roads will be fine, no problems there. Flat surface, no scale issues to consider.' His voice takes on a slightly dreamy quality. 'Houses,' he says. 'They'll be pretty big too.'

'There are no houses. It's a mountain scene.'

He nods. 'I see. Mountains should be easy enough. Chicken wire frame. A few layers of papier-mâché. Or maybe modroc would be better. Mulch it up. Some pre-paint texturing with a scourer. Yes, the only challenging bit will be the trees, really. You could even use

147

real branches. Some people do. Is it a summer or winter scene?'

'Autumn. There will be no leaves.'

He nods knowingly. 'Yep, it's always the leaves that cause problems. Leaves on the track.' He chuckles. 'It's the scale inconsistency. A bit like drops of water in *Godzilla* films. It's always the drops that give the game away.'

I hand him the two boxes and the three bags of scatter material. 'Just these, then, please. I'm sure I'll figure something out, tree-wise.'

He takes the items and scans them.

As I'm handing my card over, my phone rings: *Home calling.* I decide not to answer it.

Gerry asks if I need glue.

'Yes,' I say.

'The normal one or the needlepoint applicator?'

'What's the difference?'

'The needlepoint applicator is for fine detail. Like Superglue.'

'Is there a difference in price?'

My phone stops ringing.

'It's £1.99. The normal is 99p.'

'I'll take the needlepoint one.'

'Do you need a bag?'

'No. I'm fine.'

✷ ✷ ✷

I'm in Brockwell Park. I've stopped off to eat a filled pitta I picked up at Gabi's Deli on Charing Cross Road.

I'm sitting on a bench by the small pond, watching the birds. It could rain later. The light has changed, it seems steely.

A woman on the bench to my left is staring out across the water at the small island in the middle of the pond where most of the large birds are gathering. My feeling is that something bad has happened to everyone here today. There's a look of exhaustion on their faces.

Park as refuge. The Victorians knew what they were doing when they designed them. Sit by a pond and breathe your sadness across the water. Walk out your secrets among trees. Four moorhens are making their way towards the island, but when an exhausted looking old man stops by the low railings to throw them a shower of bread, they U-turn and head for it.

I take out the Mini kit and place it on my knee. I unwrap the filled pitta but find I no longer have the appetite for it (11 a.m. is way too early for cold ochre and spinach).

I glance over at the children's play area and spot the woman from the zebra crossing pushing her little boy on the swings. She's wearing a three quarter length leather coat and brown suede boots. Her hair is loose and straightened again. The park is suddenly transformed.

I get up and walk over to the yellow and blue surrounding fence. 'Hi,' I shout.

She turns my way. 'Oh, hi. How are you?' She says something to her little boy and heads my way. She's eating something, stuffing the last bit of it in her mouth, and when she gets up close I see the wrapper in her hand. Dark chocolate Bounty.

'What happened the other day?' she says, chewing unselfconsciously. 'Was everything okay with Mr Doran?'

'Yes, he was fine. He wasn't even at home. He'd gone out shopping.'

'Well at least you did the right thing.' She swallows with a loud gulp and looks over her shoulder at her little boy. 'I haven't done this with him in ages. Naughty of me to keep him home for no reason. We're pulling a sicky together. We've been watching DVDs and eating popcorn all morning, but we needed some fresh air. Back to the real world tomorrow.'

'And what do you do, in the real world?'

'I work in a law firm,' she says. 'And my name's Faye.' She grins confidently.

'Sorry. I always forget to introduce myself. I'm David. So you're a lawyer. Pretty stressful, I imagine.'

She shakes her head. 'No, I studied law but never finished my training contract.' She flicks her head towards her son. 'He came along, and I'm glad he did. I think I'd have hated being a lawyer. I just do the admin stuff. Property law mainly. I don't mind. It isn't that bad. I spend half my day emailing friends, the rest of the time fantasising about what it would be like to live in some of the houses we deal with.' Her eyes lock onto the model car kit, which I've only just realised is tucked under my arm. 'Didn't you say you didn't have any kids?'

'It's actually for Mr Doran. I'm helping him build a model.'

'That's sweet.'

'It's of a place he remembers from childhood,' I say. 'An important place.'

'Sounds interesting.' She looks me straight in the eyes, and again I notice the thing with her irises, the lighter brown circles around them. 'Well, if you need any help, we're just around the corner. Little man over there, he'd love to see your model. He loves anything like that. I'd best get back to him. He'll have a thousand questions — who's that? What were you talking about? What's his name? How do you know him?'

I laugh. 'Okay. Well, see you soon, I hope.'

She smiles. 'Me too.'

I walk back to the bench and sit down. I open the box and as I'm unfolding the instructions, my mobile rings. *Home calling.*

This time I take it. 'Hi,' I say.

'Where are you?'

'In the park. I just got back from the model shop. I — '

'Clare died twenty minutes ago.'

'Oh God,' I say. 'Oh God.' The hairs on my arms bristle. My scalp tightens.

'My mother's already at the hospice. I'm going to head over there now.'

'I'll come with you. I'll be home in a minute.'

'Okay. I'll wait for you. Hurry up though.'

Faye and her little boy wave as they head out of the play area. I feign a smile and wave back. I throw the pitta in the bin beside the bench. Then I sit quietly, staring at the instruction leaflet, my gaze drifting and eventually falling onto a six-step guide for the application of transfers: (1) Remove all dust from model. (2) Cut translucent films along coloured lines. (3) Soak in water for 30 seconds . . . Towards the bottom of the sheet is a line drawing of two girls, one on a scooter, another holding a tennis racket. Two boys with satchels wait nearby — Optional Extras: 1/24 scale Campus Friends Set.

In their final moments, do the dying know

the whereabouts of *their* friends and family? Do they network everyone together — a collective goodbye — connect them by invisible wires and send along a last glimmer of awareness, fizzing and sparking at each makeshift joint? Bzzt. Mum here by the bed. Bzzt. Greg mowing a lawn. Bzzt. Pippa eating a sandwich. Bzzt. Mark spitting chewing gum into the gutter. Bzzt. Niyaneke helping an African child haul a full pail of water up to the mouth of a well. Bzzt. Sarah doing yoga. Bzzzzzzzzt. David buying glue for a model, discussing with Gerry which type would best suit, thinking, 'Yes, the extra pound is worth it, a neater job all round.'

I fold the instruction sheet and put it back in the box. I replace the lid and stare down at its full-colour illustration. A painted midday sun is casting the Mini's shadow across lime green grass, a shadow that will stay that shape and size forever, never lengthen, never make it to the nearby tree.

12

Clare has been dead for just over an hour by the time Sarah and I are walking side by side down the corridor towards her room. Her door is open and I can hear her mother's low talking.

Not quite ready to face what's in there, I pause in front of a window. Sarah walks on. I look down at the car park. Was the ivy-covered wall always so low, the orange fruits or berries so bright? The monkey puzzle tree seems to sprawl, its branches fuller. The houses opposite appear further away. Is the wooden bench in the corner new?

Sarah's mother is sitting by the bed when I enter Clare's room a few minutes later. Her back blocks my view of her dead daughter's face. She hears me come in but doesn't turn around. I approach the foot of the bed and stand next to Sarah. I can see Clare now. Her eyes are open slightly. Her skin is waxy. Her purple crocheted cap is on the pillow next to her ear.

Her mother sniffs. 'No more pain.' She lets her head fall forwards until her forehead touches Clare's smooth looking left hand, which she's holding in both of hers.

'Were you with her?' I ask.

'Yes, I was wetting a towel. She just sighed and went.'

'It's nice that you were here,' Sarah says.

Her mother dabs at her eyes with a handkerchief. 'Yes.' She looks at us. 'Do you want to spend some time alone with her? I think she'd like that. Go and get a drink. I'll be down in five minutes.'

We nod in unison.

Sarah spends half an hour with Clare while I sit in the cafe with her mum. We hardly say a word. Then it's my turn.

I go back up, close the door behind me and sit by the bed. Clare's arms are by her side, bare and above the blanket, put there, I imagine, by Sarah, or maybe a nurse. Her mouth is open slightly. Her bottom lip droops. She looks young and at the same time very old. Her ribcage is still. No rise. No fall. Any moment now she'll jump at me. 'Boo!'

I stroke her forearm for a while. Then, once I've gathered up some courage, I slip my hand under hers. Already she's icy cold, and I squeeze her hand knowing how pointless it is.

Without feeling in any way self-conscious, I start to talk to her. I tell her all about the model, describe the scene, the road, the small lake, the mountains we'll build. 'It'll be a bit like your green drawing of South Africa,' I say. 'That one up there on the wall. I'm going to ask your mother if I can have it. I'm not sure why I like it so much, but I do.' I let go of her hand and pick up the crocheted cap, which I fold in half and put back on the pillow. Then I stand and absently search through a stack of clothes that are neatly folded on her chair.

Unsure of where to put myself, I then do the opposite of what I actually want to do: I sit down again, lean forward and place my hand on her forehead. It feels skinless and hard, like damp wood. I reach towards her mouth and touch the tip of my finger to her bottom lip. Most of her blood has already left it, and the bruising where she used to bite down on it shows clearly now. I press gently, trying to push the lip back up over her teeth. It won't give, so I take my hand away.

★　★　★

Half an hour later we are gathered together in the room next door. I'm leaning against the sink. Sarah's sitting on a green plastic chair by the bedside cabinet. Her mother is talking — while looking at the sickly pink wall behind me — about the wording of an obituary. I hear little of what she's saying

156

because I'm wondering when the old man whose room this was — the one whose rattling breath I'd often hear in the corridor as I was on the way to kitchen — died. Sometimes I'd look in here and see him propped up on pillows in his blue pyjamas. An old man and a young woman as neighbours. That's just not right.

Sarah's mother is now saying that it would be nice if one of us could compose something. And perhaps we could find a poem to read out at the church. I stand and walk over to the window. 'Does anyone mind if I open this? It's stuffy in here.' No-one answers. I open it and cool air wafts in. I look down at Sarah's Mini. It looks tiny. Like a model. 1/24 scale.

Only two hours ago I was talking to Faye in the park. We were laughing and joking and talking about nothing in particular. I picture her and her son in a café, drinking hot chocolate with pink and white marshmallows bobbing on top. Then at home later, in her teal-coloured kitchen, cooking up high-carb, high protein, Caribbean comfort stodge.

Sarah's mother has had an idea. Christina Rossetti's *Remember me* would be a good choice.

Sarah nods. 'Yes, I like that poem.'

Her mother looks at me. 'David?'

I nod too.

Everything has been said, arrangements discussed, and the three of us are busy back in Clare's room. We move around her quietly. I volunteer to clear out the fridge. The two Ski yoghurts still occupy the same position, top shelf, their lids more swollen now, threatening to burst at any time. I drop them into a black bin liner. A hardened piece of cheese and some wrinkled apples are the next to go. Then some German Pumpernickel wrapped in silver foil. The two chocolate éclairs don't slide off the paper plate when I tilt it, so I drop the whole thing in. Everything goes in the liner apart from a gold, unopened box of Belgian Pralines. I place them on the worktop among Clare's cards. 'Does anyone want these or the juice or the milk?' No-one does. I drop all three into the liner and tie the top.

Sarah's mother steps up on a chair and begins carefully peeling Clare's drawings from the wall. 'Would anyone like any of these?'

'I'd like the green one,' I say. 'If that's okay.' I look at Sarah. She's at the sink, a bunch of withered tulips in one hand, a half-full vase of green water in the other. 'Unless you'd like to have it.'

She shakes her head. 'No. You've always liked it.'

Sarah's mother frowns down at me, confused. 'Why do you two always talk as though you're not really a couple? It will look lovely in your flat. Share it.'

Sarah pours the green water down the sink and drops the tulips in the bin.

'It's Johannesburg,' her mother says. 'A rally she once went to in the mountains. She never finished it.'

'I like it the way it is.'

'You could finish it for her.'

'No, I wouldn't dream of doing that.'

She peels the drawing from the wall and studies it. She blows on it and brushes at it with her hand. The centre of her brow raises in exactly the same way Sarah's does. 'It really is a pity she didn't finish it though. Don't you think?'

★　★　★

By three in the afternoon all is taken care of. Our cars are loaded up with bin liners and we go back to reception to say our goodbyes. The nurse tells us that Clare will be moved to the basement, which I assume means cold storage. We thank her for everything, then leave for the last time.

Without really knowing where I'm heading, I drive past the street we live on and then find myself heading for Brockwell Park again (it's the only place that seems right). We manage to find a space in the Lido car park — the last one — and I pull in and stop.

There's some kind of event going on in this half of the park. A mini festival. A small stage is being erected half way up the grassy slope. There are stalls selling clothes and food. Faye could still be here.

For a few minutes, Sarah and I sit staring through the windscreen in silence.

There's a handwritten sign on the Lido door: SORRY. NO YOGA THIS EVENING. :(

'Do you want to go and see what's going on?' I ask.

Sarah shrugs. 'I don't mind.'

'You decide.'

'No. I don't want to make decisions right now.'

'Are you in the mood for people?'

'I don't know what I'm in the mood for. I don't care. You?'

'Not really. But I'm easy either way.'

'What a fuck up,' she says.

I nod in agreement.

'I don't mean today. I mean everything. You don't know the half of it.' She opens the door. 'Come on. Ignore me. Since we're here we may as well walk.'

We head into the park and begin our ascent

to the café. Half way up the slope, Sarah stops at a stall and buys a pair of what look like yellow, child's sunglasses, which she puts on. Further up, near the tennis courts, we find a reasonably quiet spot and sit down.

'So,' I say. 'What now?'

'I said I'd go and help sort through Clare's clothes later.'

'Do you want me to come with you?'

'No, it's okay.'

'Are you sure? I don't mind.'

'I'm sure,' she says. 'I'll go on my own.' A white frisbee lands close to her hand, and she looks at it as though it's the first frisbee she's ever seen in her life. A chunky, red-faced girl comes running over and picks it up. 'Sorry,' she says breathlessly. She jogs away, throwing the frisbee mid-stride.

'Shall we move somewhere else?'

Sarah lies down on her back. 'No. I'm fine here.' She brushes a strand of hair away from her mouth. 'When you were up with Clare, and I was down in the café, my mum was telling me about how she was feeding her crushed ice from the machine this morning, just before she died. She was only semiconscious, but she suddenly reached out both hands and said, 'Help me.' She said it twice.'

'Do you feel bad that you weren't there with her?'

Sarah shakes her head. 'Not really.' She sits up suddenly and takes off the sunglasses. 'Should we go?'

'We only just got here.'

'Should we be here, though, in a park? It feels wrong to be lying on grass. Maybe there's something else we should be doing, or somewhere we should be. Maybe we're not doing the thing we're supposed to on the day someone dies. What did you do after your mum died?'

I raise my knees and brush grass from the backs of my thighs. 'Took the dog out for a walk. It was five o'clock in the morning by the time everything had been sorted out. I phoned you. Don't you remember?'

'Of course. I mean later. For the rest of the day.'

'Not much. In the evening I went to the pub with my dad.'

Sarah looks at me, a look of puzzlement on her face. 'I'm an only child,' she says. 'This morning I wasn't, and now, just like that, I am.' She sighs heavily, pauses to think, then says, 'How's Pete's leg?'

'He'll be in the cast for six to eight weeks.'

'What about the model?'

'A nonstarter.'

'You need to help him make it. It's important.'

'Not in comparison to this.'

'It is. You have to do it.'

'Sarah, you've just lost your sister. Believe me, that can wait.'

'I'm not a bad person,' she suddenly blurts out.

'Who said you were?'

'I just need you to know that. I might have made mistakes, misjudged things, badly, but that doesn't mean I'm a bad person.' She shakes her head. 'It's not right that you still don't know.'

'Know what?'

'He should have told you by now. It wasn't meant to go on for this long. If something more serious had happened to him when he had his fall, it would have been shitty for you to find out some other way. I know you never believed any of what I told you about him. I know you're not stupid. I just didn't want to have to be the one to tell you the truth. But maybe I should have. Fuck! Maybe I should tell you now. I can't believe I'm having to do this on top of everything else.'

'Sarah,' I say, 'whatever it is he's told you, I wouldn't take it too seriously. It's probably nonsense. He's all over the place at the moment. One day he's fine and talking about doing something that will 'be good for us', the next day he throws himself from a bus.

He'll probably need hospitalising sooner or later. Who knows what's going on in his head at the moment?'

Sarah looks at me, her eyes the saddest I've ever seen them all day. 'If anyone does, it will be you,' she says. 'You're his brother.'

II

13

'Jesus Christ!', 'What were you thinking?', 'Are you out of your fucking mind?'

These were the kind of things I shouted at Sarah as we argued our way around the park that afternoon, which felt pretty harrowing under the circumstances. Over and over again I pointed out that it wasn't so much the outcome, but the way she'd steered me towards it, the sheer willpower it must have taken to keep something so huge from me all this time. At one point I even brought Clare into it, Clare who had only been dead a matter of hours. The hints she'd dropped about Sarah's past, and how even she, with so little to lose, had managed to avoid resorting to gossip.

Sarah told me everything then. What did it matter now anyway? She told me about the time she'd spent in a treatment centre for eating disorders in her teens. One deception after another. How she'd smear the butter they were given at meal times on her forearms, and then roll her sleeves down to hide it. How she used to make a piece of fruit last for three or four hours. How she'd drink ice cold water to burn off negative calories, or sleep naked without a duvet and the heating turned off so that she'd shiver. Punch herself in the stomach whenever it rumbled to make it stop, and hurt too much to be able to eat anyway. One time, after leaving the centre and coming home, she went out on a bike ride because she could see her mum preparing lunch. She called after half an hour to say she'd had an accident, and when her dad arrived to pick her up she'd kicked the bike's front wheel out of shape, bought a sandwich, and appeared to be eating the last bite of it (she'd already thrown the rest away).

Hearing all this, I felt sorry for her. But I also had to be realistic with myself. Did I want to be dealing with that kind of thing, maybe for the rest of my life?

The next two days were hard. I was torn between doing the right thing (helping out with funeral preparations) and what I actually wanted to do (spend time alone to consider the weight of everything I'd been told).

Finally we called a truce, but nothing was achieved or resolved. No explanation in the world, not even the fact that Sarah had just lost her only sister, was enough to change my mind about what I needed to do.

Move out for a while and do some thinking.

Sarah is a good person underneath her snappy, defensive ways. She hates her sharp tongue just as much as I do. She probably thought she was doing the right thing, probably pictured a Hollywood style ending. The two long-lost brothers with tears in their eyes. They hug, the music swells, and she gets a mention in the credits. It makes no difference that she orchestrated the whole thing to help us out. I tried to allow it to, but I just couldn't. It felt wrong to continue living with someone who was essentially sent into my life as a spy and kept up the lie from day one.

And so convincingly.

I don't doubt that the story of how *we* met — our base coat and primer — would hush even the most riveting dinner party. Some might say that it is, in its own way, romantic. Unfortunately, I fail to see it for anything other than what it really is — a fucked-up mess.

So . . .

I started phoning around, and on only the fourth call I struck it lucky with an old friend, Jane, who was going away for three weeks and needed someone to cat-sit. Jane lives on a boat in Chelsea harbour, a 39ft Dutch river cruiser called West Star Rising. I jumped at the chance.

But it didn't turn out to be quite the break I expected. The first morning, I woke up feeling dead to the world. Unable to drag myself out of bed, I called in sick and told Phil it was unlikely I'd be able to see Pete for at least a week, maybe even longer.

'Take it easy and don't worry,' he said. 'Someone else will stand in for you.'

Again I considered telling him everything. But again I didn't. Instead, I went back to bed and lay there going over it all.

★   ★   ★

My parents met through a car accident. They got married, got pregnant, and gave the baby away because he was disabled. Then they split up. Two years later, out of guilt and, in all likelihood, the belief that no-one else in their right mind would have them, they got back together, decided to replace what they'd lost, and I came into the world. Not exactly the stuff of fairy tales.

I've been upended by my own backstory. Everything I thought was this, has turned out, instead, to be that. What are you supposed to do when that happens, when you find out it's all a sham? One morning, there you are, you get up, stretch, lose your balance a bit, and when you lean on the wall to steady yourself it falls over, followed in turn by the other three — boof, boof, boof. And there you stand, an actor in a role you thought you'd perfected, one you'd had a whole lifetime to grow into — there you stand, out in the open, everything either flattened or fake — like Buster Keaton, or poor old Jim Carey in *The Truman Show* when the tip of his boat tears a hole in the painted-on sky.

* * *

Sarah breezed into my exhibition that evening last November. Why? Because she wanted to buy a painting? Because there's nothing she likes more of an evening than to go uninvited to private views? No, it turns out that she breezed in because she was working with a mentally ill man who she was fond of, not in *that* way, just fond of, and said man had told her, over the years, about his appalling life. He'd now decided that he'd prefer if it didn't go on for too much longer. Before he ends it, though, and he's fine with that, sure about it, has long since come to terms with it, there's one final thing he needs to do. He's always known that he has a brother (his father told him the names of his birth mother and father when he was growing up) and he's been thinking he might like to find him, just to see

171

what he's like. Sarah agrees to help. She thinks it will give him a good reason to want to stay alive.

Her performance at the opening was incredible. I'll give her that much. She played the Cancer card and hooked me well and truly in. The two of us had a meeting of minds, shared head nods. 'Yes, I know how you feel. Difficult, isn't it? Such an unpredictable illness. Uncertainty on top of uncertainty. Blah blah blah . . . '

Meanwhile, so-called psychic Pete was probably pacing up and down his living room, waiting for the phone call, which eventually came: 'He's an interesting guy. You'll like him. I think it went well . . . '

But how did the two of them even get that far? A family detective? No, it turns out that it was much simpler than that.

Just over six months ago, Pete and Sarah began eliminating Price after Price on Google. They finally found artist David Price. Instinctively, and despite the fact that there was virtually no physical resemblance whatso-ever, Pete somehow knew that this David Price was the one. No doubt about it. He saw something in the painting style that seemed familiar, in a way he couldn't quite explain (something about the choice of colours; was that it?). Sarah then suggested the exhibition as first point of contact, followed by feedback on what he was like. As it turned out, he was okay, seemed nice, this David Price. He even said he'd think about starting as a volunteer at Lady Gomm.

High fives all round that evening, I imagine. Plans rarely come together like that one.

Next comes the 250 mile train journey. The stakeout under the hedge. The staring up at the window of the woman who gave him away when he was born. Fuck her. Fuck them both. The creeping around the back of the house and peering in through the window. His knuckles rest on the glass, but then he loses his nerve and decides not to knock. Back on the train. Morning. Lunch with the man in the white string vest and shorts. Hovering soup bowl. Whispers in the street. Abandoned swimming trips. Conversations with a mosaic of Jesus' face. Merry Christmas to me. The bus coming up the road. Wait . . . wait . . . wait . . .

Now.

Next, as we already know, artist (and complete mug) David Price (lets call him ADP for short) does volunteer, and before long he has a job that will bring him face to face with his brother, his mentally ill and fresh out of hospital brother, his not-yet-but-soon-will-be arsonist brother. What's more, the two of them will get on reasonably well. They'll share an interest in art (of course), and before long ADP will be in his brother's kitchen peeling potatoes.

Sarah, by this time, not intentionally, and it would be fair to say not entirely with Pete's blessing, has fallen for ADP. It's an awkward situation for all three parties (slightly less so for ADP as he's the only one who doesn't have a fucking clue what's going on).

For the next two months Sarah continues relaying information about ADP's private life, which is, of course, in a way, also Pete's life.

Details. Facts. When's and where's. Still so many questions. The Google search. Did he look at my paintings via the gallery website? Is that were he saw the *Cut by Grass* series? Or did he actually go along there in person and ask to see anything they might still have of mine, have the attendant wheel out the portfolio, lean a few canvasses against the wall? If I were a writer, these would be things I'd be keen to get right. I'd do the research, cross-check facts, run the Google search on myself to see where it led.

The truth is, I'm just not that interested. I'm not an ins and outs man. Maybe he has an old Quality Street tin full to the brim with bits and bobs, trinkets, the tarnished silver ring I mysteriously lost a while ago, pins, cotton reels, photographs, my old NHS card — a birth certificate. For all I know, he has the lot, the whole package, hard evidence (if that's what you want to call it). Maybe ever since he was a small boy our paths have been converging, me clueless, him always aware (except, of course, for on his cloud cuckoo land days).

Then crash. We collide. Third time lucky.

So what? Who cares? Where will it get me to know all there is to know? Great, pin it down, draw up a chart, arrows from this to that, circles here, underlining there. That he did find me by Googling the name. That when he came across David Price the artist, he might have thought to himself: 'That's what I'd liked to have done, given the chance.'

I'm willing to accept all of the above as the truth. No further questions.

He's my brother and I'm his. It's plain to see (now that I've been told). When Sarah just came out with it so casually in the park, the strange thing is, I didn't for a second doubt that it was true. If anything, it was suddenly glaringly obvious, and I felt like a complete idiot for not having seen it sooner. Gestures. Certain expressions. His laugh. The way he sits in a chair. Even the way he takes his tea.

Yes, we are brothers, of course. But all the hard evidence in the world, all the filled in gaps, all the talking, none of it will alter that fact. It will all just be decoration. Add Ons. Yes, I'm angry about all that lost time. No, he may not be the long-lost brother everyone dreams of.

★　★　★

It's day three in the harbour and things have got a little better. The sun has come out, and today I've spent less time going over the events of the last four months and more time up on deck trying to be present. Despite several missed calls from Sarah, and fifteen from my brother, my mind has returned to a reasonably clutter-free state.

★　★　★

On day four, though, as soon as I wake up I can feel the heaviness is back. Last night I reread the suicide handout and understood, for the first time, references that up until now had remained a mystery. The Him (and I'm fairly certain this was meant to be misleading) isn't God at all, but me. The journey, the quest, was the trip up north to stare at the bedroom window — 'Her light before it went out' — from his vantage point among the brambles. And letter #2, the Gothic script poem, clearly constructed around how my (our) parents met — *two bright lights up-end the world, bringing an infant into being, who is not the chosen one* — I feel an idiot for not having decoded. But then I never really saw the point to poetry, always failed to understand why anyone would deliberately veil meaning when they could simply remove all the unnecessary capitals and put the lines back together to make straightforward prose.

I eat breakfast thinking about my mother.

Death is strange. And people deal with it in such different ways. Sarah, for example, hangs on to the things she can control, like her weight, washing up methods, and insistence that everyone takes off their shoes before coming into the house. These things make her feel safe when all around her isn't.

If anything I'm probably the opposite.

Small things don't bother me at all since my mother died (let's be honest, war was never declared because someone forgot to put away the mop bucket). I no longer worry about money (though I rarely have much), my own health seems pretty unimportant, and this year I've car-booted half my worldly possessions according to the following rule: If I haven't worn, read, played, or used it in the last six months — bin liner.

A stripped back life.

I'm Jack London in the *Klondike*, Werner Herzog's *Grizzly Man*, Rip Van Winkle, the kid from *Into the Wild*. The city is no longer the place for me. All I need is the trickle of a stream, the rise and fall of the sun, a diet of wild berries, root vegetables and fresh fish.

This probably sounds like a crisis of sorts, a rock bottom, but to be honest I'm hoping I've had that already. If so, all I can say is this: it was brief, dramatic, and as close to sheer terror as anything I've ever experienced (including my street corner dementia episode).

It happened on New Years Eve. Sarah and I were still up north with my dad. My mother had only been dead for twelve days and what was I doing? Flicking through a copy of *New Scientist* I'd found lying around. I came across an article about a 'body farm' in Texas where studies were being carried out into the decomposition of human remains. A journalist had gone to the 'farm' to write about it, and she'd seen bodies strewn here and there, swollen and black, some under trees, one next to a wooden fence. The 5 stages of decay were described in detail: 1: Autolysis (self-digestion): the body's enzymes (fluids) begin eating through the cells. 2: Gloving: the skin on the hands loosens, forming what look like transparent gloves. 3: Bloating: the body fills up with gases. 4: Dissolving: the organs turn to yellow soup. 5: Consumption: whatever remains is eaten by beetles.

The End.

Sarah didn't want to read the article, and what's more she was pretty sure I shouldn't be reading it either. I turned to her at one point. 'There are so many ways to die, but only one of being dead.'

'I think you should put that away now,' she said. 'What will your dad think if he sees you reading it?'

Morbidly fascinated, though, and hoping I might at some point be able to do something creative with what I was reading, I continued.

Until my throat began to tighten. Until my heart started to pound so violently it felt like an *external* organ — like it was giant and swollen and on top of me, weighing me down. I got up and walked around for a bit, but every movement I made seemed pre-programmed and robotic. Whatever I did had a rhythm to it. It's hard to explain exactly what I mean. My fingers felt huge, like salamis, and whenever I turned my head it was as though I was turning it in slow motion. Not like being stoned. Different to that. I thought I was having a heart attack, checked for stroke symptoms. Arm okay. No slurred speech. I looked in the mirror to see if my mouth had sagged to one side. It hadn't.

I started to cry at my reflection.

Due credit to Sarah. She remained calm the whole time. She talked me down and only later informed me that what I'd had was probably a panic attack. Others might follow. She'd had plenty in her life.

★ ★ ★

I'm lying in the sun. I've been lying in the sun the whole afternoon. It feels good to do nothing. I'm not taking a break from some demanding activity, not allowing a meal to go down, not waiting for paint to dry. I'm simply lying in the sun and enjoying it.

Last night I sketched out my initials, nautically themed. Then I sketched out a reversed version for Pete.

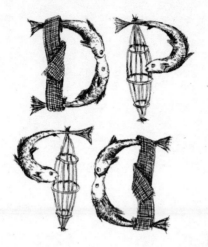

Back to Back
Pen on paper 160 x 90 cm

I reach for my phone and dial his number. He answers after only half a ring.

'It's me,' I say. 'Just listen. Let me talk. I know the whole story now. I'm sorry I haven't been around — I needed some time to mull things over. I've done that now. I'll be back on Monday morning, but this is how I want to play it. I want to make the model. I just want to get on with it, drink tea, and not talk about anything, not yet. I haven't talked to dad yet, because I'm too angry with him and don't have the faintest idea what to say. I will talk to you, though, in time, if that's what you want, but not yet. Okay? Do we have a deal?'

'Yes,' he says. 'Deal. See you on Monday . . . little brother.'

14

Car Crash 1984
1/24 Scale, mixed media on marine ply

We will need:

Four foldable tressles. One 8' × 4" sheet of 18mm ply. Electric drill and jigsaw. Plastic sheeting. Staple gun. Silicone sealant (brown or clear). Gravel (the fine type used in aquariums). Modroc bandage. Chicken wire. Newspaper. Wallpaper paste. A bucket. Marker pens. Paint — black, white, greens and various earth colours. Two 1/24 scale self-assembly model-kits. A handsaw, hammer, tape measure, pliers, tin snips and file. Sandpaper. Scissors. Gaffer tape. A Pritt stick?

I prop the ply on the four tressles and sketch out the shape of the lake. I drill a 10mm hole inside the line, cut out the hole, and sand away the sharp edges. The fine-gauge chicken wire I moulded into a bowl shape earlier, with an overhanging rim around it, a bit like an upturned sunhat, fits snugly after some shaping, stretching and bending. I staple it in place and hammer any sharp strands flat.

182

For the next three hours I cover the inside of the bowl shape with layer upon layer of modroc bandage. By lunchtime it's dry and still warm from the chemical reaction of hardening. I rap on it with my knuckles and it makes a satisfying sound. The lake could hold up to ten pints of water, but then it could easily be more.

I go out into the garden and look up at the sky. It's overcast and the air smells faintly of fires. I think about Clare's funeral. She'll be cremated. That's what she wanted. I'll be there, despite everything that's happened. It's only right.

I miss her.

I walk towards the house, and halfway there I spot him through the open kitchen door, my strange looking older brother wheeled up close to the table, his red cast leg resting on the stool I put there for him. The Mini and VW Camper kit are on the table in front of him.

It suddenly occurs to me that what we've agreed to do together is my apology to him. Not that it's me who owes him one. Still, using my skills, over the next fourteen days (roughly how long we'll need) I'll do all I can to make up for the fact that I had my life and he ended up with his.

I enter the kitchen.

'Which one will be easiest to make?'

183

'The Mini,' I say. 'There are probably less parts.'

He picks up one of the tyres, slips it onto his finger, then holds his hand out in front like a soon-to-be bride in a jewellers shop. 'Okay, I'll start it this afternoon.'

Two hours later I'm already building up the ground areas so that the road will be higher than the lake. I break off and head back to the house to consult him. He's been watching TV and frowns when I walk in.

I roll the empty wheelchair to one side and lower myself into an armchair. 'What's on?'

'A documentary about a doctor at Great Ormond Street hospital who operates on babies while they're still in the womb.'

We watch in silence as the surgeon pushes a long needle into a woman's swollen stomach, the voice-over explaining that fluid needs to be drained from the baby's chest, if it's to survive. I gasp in disbelief at the ultrasound image, the baby instinctively moving away from the needle as it nears its chest. I inhale sharply as the white outline of skin resists and gives way. It's in. The doctor's face fills the screen. He's Greek and looks tired.

Pete switches to BBC One, *Traffic Cops*, and I say nothing. Odd that he'd want to watch sick babies, and now *this* — cars speeding, fishtailing, crashing and rolling over.

He laughs out loud as a Formula I car hits

a barrier, flips over and sends a shower of sparks towards the crowd.

I ask him about the ground. How flat does he want it? Does he want undulations? If so, how many? Does he want ditches? Does he want fences? Does he want lay-bys? What about hedges?

Cigarette pointed at the TV, he stutters out smoke. 'Not too flat. Undulations, some. Ditches, no. Fences, yes. Lay-bys, one.'

'I seem to be doing this alone, Pete. Are you going to make a start on the car or not?'

'In a minute.'

I stand up to leave the room but get waylaid by Police helicopter footage of a stolen silver BMW heading down the motorway at 120 miles an hour. I laugh in disbelief as it weaves between other cars that appear, in comparison, to be crawling along. I shake my head as it takes the slip road and the chase continues down country lanes before ending in a farmyard, where the thief jumps out and tries to hide behind a barn, unaware, it seems, of the helicopter circling above.

Pete cackles hysterically.

★ ★ ★

Later, as he dozes on the sofa under the fleecy blanket I brought from the bedroom, I cut the plastic sheeting into a large circle and try it for size in the lake bowl. I coat it with silicone and press it down. Using more of the modroc bandage, I blend the chicken wire fringe and board together.

End of day one.

I call Iris and tell her that I'll be checking in on Pete over the weekend. She tells me that she'll do the same. I head back to the boat.

★ ★ ★

On Monday, once I've set him up with breakfast, I use the wire-cutters to nip off large squares of chicken wire. Taking my time, I form irregular but modest ground features — small rolling hills, lake bank, and mounds that trees will grow from. Working from the lake upwards, I knit the chicken wire squares together, slope up a few inches, dip, then rise until I reach my marker-pen guidelines. Chicken wire and modroc probably won't do for the road. I may need something flatter. Six inch wide strips cut from a cereal box?

I find one on top of the fridge. The card is perfect, the grey not as daunting as white. By lunchtime things are really taking shape.

Midafternoon and I've laid a second section of road — two ten inch lengths of card — and am studying the mountains. The larger of the two suddenly reminds me of the one in Clare's green drawing, and at that point I find myself wondering about the funeral. Is my charity shop, pinstriped suit appropriate? Will I be asked to read something? Will Sarah's mother get all the way through the Christina Rossetti poem without breaking down? Who will speak first during the journey from the church to the crematorium, and to say what? At the time of committal, will the curtain move smoothly, or jerk, maybe even get stuck? Has that ever happened? Who maintains the machinery and are they paid well for the responsibility? Are the ashes you're given really those of your loved one?

I study the chicken wire frame and find it impossible to picture mountains, feel their bulk. Do they look too big or too small? I can't decide. If I cover them with a thin layer of papier-mâché I'll probably get a better sense of them. I mix the wallpaper paste thick and gloopy. Then I head for the living room to look for newspaper.

But I find something else instead.

His head is tilted back. His eyes are open but blind to the world. He's very pale, his cheeks sunken, and on the pillow near his mouth there's a small amount of red-brown dribble that's hopefully tea. I call for an ambulance, and as I give the required information I pat his cheek gently, lift his wrist to feel for a pulse, look for external signs, indications of what might have happened. I spot a brown, coin-sized stain on the white sheet where it dips and forms a smooth valley between his legs. Carefully I pull the sheet back. The stench of shit overpowers me. I reel away from the sofa and vomit on the carpet.

I set about tidying up. I need to get things straight. The bulk of the shit is mostly treacle-black, a central pile surrounded by a light brown stain flecked with red. Eyes watering, gagging, I part his legs and attempt to scoop the shit onto a piece of card. I retch again but nothing comes up.

I spread a clean sheet out on the floor and lift him from the sofa. His good leg flops limply. The cast one is more of a problem. He's much heavier than I thought he'd be, and I struggle to stay balanced as I lower him to the floor. I bend my knees, the way I've been taught. A back injury is the last thing I need.

Kneeling over him, my curiosity gets the better of me. I peel away the waistband of his red and navy Y-fronts and follow the short, light brown scar that runs from his naval to just above his thinning pubic hair. I wince at the plastic tube that enters the base of his penis — a tiny stub, the excess bunched-together foreskin resembling a miniature, age-yellowed cabbage. In the tube that drains pinky yellow urine to the half-full bag strapped to his thigh are tiny bubbles. His scrotum is fairly normal in size, but hairless.

I gather the corners and edges of the soiled bed sheet together. With some twisting and folding, I make a parcel of the shit and blood and stuff it into a bin liner. I tie the top once. Then again.

Next I scoop my vomit (mainly tea and muesli) onto the TV guide, half covering the faces of two actresses I vaguely recognise from a series about the goings-on in a hair salon. I bend the magazine to form a U-shaped channel. Sloping it, damming one end with my left hand, feeling the lukewarm vomit against my palm, I head for the bathroom, watching the tea and muesli ebb gently back and forth.

The vomit down the toilet, the TV guide in the bin, I fill a bowl with water and washing powder. Back in the living room, down on my hands and knees, I scrub at the carpet, thinking about how much he'd hate to see this — this mess of brotherly body fluids. I work up a lather, rinse with cold water, and find that the cleaned patch is much brighter than the rest of the carpet. He won't like that, won't like it at all, but it's too late to do anything about it, the ambulance is here.

At the hospital I wait for an hour in A&E to see a nurse. Finally, one comes out and tells me the bad news. He's bled internally. I tell her that I already gathered that much and press for further details. There are good nurses. There are bad nurses. There are nurses who, tired and overworked, occasionally let their guard down and say way too much. She isn't one of them. She's professional, stands her ground, has good solid boundaries. 'There isn't much point in staying,' she says. 'Family only, I'm afraid.'

'I am family.'

'You said you were his carer.'

'Did I?'

'Yes.'

'I'm also his brother.'

'Okay,' she says. 'Come back tomorrow. In the afternoon. We'll know more then.'

I go outside.

Phil.

Norma.

Iris.

These are the three people I need to inform.

The care manager.

The absent sister.

The ex-wife/best friend/thief.

I switch on my phone.

I call Phil first, and he tells me to come in for supervision tomorrow. I mentally pencil it in. 10 a.m. Tuesday. Office.

I call Norma but it goes straight to voicemail.

I call Iris. And while it's ringing I promise myself that I'll put our differences to one side.

As I explain what's happened, she's all tuts and sighs, puffs and pants, but I don't lose my cool, I don't want to give her the satisfaction.

When she begins talking me through her movements, I hold the phone away from my ear in order not to hear 'I'm putting my coat on' and 'I can't find my purse' and 'Where's my purse, John?' 'John?' I put the phone back to my ear and say, 'Iris, listen.' But she doesn't. 'John, where's my purse? John! . . . Are you there?' I repeat her name. Again. Again. But then I hear the clunking sound as she places the receiver down on a hard surface. I have no power over her. She may not even pick it up again. She may leave it there. She may forget about it altogether.

In order not to lose my temper, I think about random things that bring comfort for one reason or another — the incomprehensible hugeness of the Blue Whale in the

Natural History museum; tangerine orange (the colour of some forms of crab); a row of brightly coloured beach huts; a postcard Clare had by her bed — *Typical Morocco* — four black and white goats up a squat tree.

Iris is now being sworn at by John. I hold the phone away from my ear. I have no wish to hear his obscenities at point blank range — 'How the fuck do I know where your fucking purse is? For fucks sake, Iris, can't you fucking keep track of anything?' When she finally does pick up again to say that she'll be there within the hour, I tell her no, they don't yet know what the problem is, and when they do they'll probably operate. 'There's been some kind of haemorrhaging. Let's meet tomorrow. Reception. Midafternoon.'

Silence. Then heavy smokers breathing. 'I might just come up there anyway. I don't want him on his own. And he won't want you there. He doesn't — '

I end day two by hanging up on her.

15

I'm at the office waiting for Phil to finish on the phone. He's sitting on the end of his desk, his free hand patting out a rhythm on his thigh. A three-high stack of large cardboard boxes stands in the middle of the room. The boxes are taped up and have dates written on them in black marker. Phil makes the 'two minutes' sign with his fingers and then silently mouths 'coffee'. I give him the thumbs up and go next door to the team room.

The other three support workers are out on visits, and as usual their desks are strewn with newspapers, visit sheets, notepads, McDonald's wrappers and paper cups. My half desk is empty except for a pencil, an orange pen/paper-clip holder, and the phone.

I make the coffees but then find there isn't any milk in the fridge. I check to see if there are any biscuits in the green jar, and there are — Gingernuts. I hear Phil laugh out loud next door. Then, for some reason, he sings the opening lines of Johnny Cash's *Ring of Fire* in a mock Welsh tenor. He laughs an unrestrained laugh, probably at himself, then says, 'You're a saint, Derv, you really are.

Thanks. I'll give it to you later.'

When I come through carrying the coffees, two Gingernuts clamped between my lips, Phil's back behind his desk, writing my name on a new page of his hardback A4 notebook. I pass him his coffee, take a bite of one of the Gingernuts, and sit down opposite him. 'What's with the boxes?'

'X-files,' he says. 'We're having a clear out. They didn't *all* die. I like to think we have had *some* success stories.' He clears his throat and pushes himself back on his wheeled office chair, patting both pockets of his jeans.

'Under your pad,' I say.

He lifts the pad with one hand and slides his tobacco from under it with the other. 'You don't mind, do you?'

I shake my head. 'Course not.'

'Good man. Chips and mushy peas.' He points a finger at me. 'That's what I'm going to have for lunch. Mary's trying to get me to eat healthily. But fuck salad, I say.'

This is Phil leading. He's a good manager, one fully aware of the value of humour. He knows how to use the 'shit sandwich': say something nice (bread), say what needs to be said (shit), say something nice again to finish (bread). He'll keep things light for a while, crack a few jokes, ease us in, maybe tell me one of his stories, a mental health anecdote or

194

something about the day-to-day perils of being a man — 'I see at least ten women a day I'd like to sleep with, but I know that even if they would entertain a middle-aged grey-haired git like me, it wouldn't make me as happy as sitting in my garden with Mary, a glass of beer in one hand, a fag in the other' — and then we'll get down to business.

A siren starts up outside, a patrol car called out from the police station opposite. The siren switches from the early, fraught whip of sound to the second phase — still loud but less threatening. Phil takes this as an opportunity to roll a cigarette, and as he does, and although he's clearly in good spirits, we sit in what to me feels like a slightly awkward silence. For the first time since I got here it suddenly occurs to me that he might know about my recent discovery. Sarah could have phoned him — they always did get on well. Or Pete could have finally told Iris, and she loves being the bearer of news, especially if it's bad.

He taps the roll-up on his desk, lights it, then theatrically slaps his lighter down on the pad. He picks up his pen. 'So. How's everything with you?'

'Not bad,' I say cautiously.

'What about your paintings? How's that all going? Sold any to Mr Saatchi recently for six-figure sums?'

The police siren is still audible but faint. I laugh. 'No.'

'Mary's started doing mosaics,' he says. 'All she ever seems to do these days is smash up tiles and bottles. I think she's ready for a baby.' One of Phil's favourite mannerisms is to rub his hands together, and he does this now, grinning mischievously. 'I think I could probably oblige, even at my age.' He exhales smoke from the corner of his mouth. 'And how's Pete?'

'So so.'

Phil nods thoughtfully. Then he picks up his coffee and looks at it. 'No milk?'

'No.'

He takes a careful sip, grimaces. 'Iris phoned me again this morning, about the fire.'

My stomach takes a roll. 'What did she say?'

'That she thinks it definitely *was* him.' He brushes ash from the corner of his desk.

'Anything else?'

'Not really. Just her usual ramblings. I don't think she's too well at the moment either. Right, let's get the boring stuff out of the way so that I can go and get my chips. Pete's bus accident (if that's really what we're to assume it was). Is there anything that you think could have been done differently, from your end?'

'I suppose I could have gone with him to the model shop. That would probably have made more sense.'

Nodding to himself, Phil begins to write. I lean forwards slightly and follow the Bic's tip as it makes its sharp little up-and-down jerks across the page. Two words jump out: *aware* and *regretfully*. Then a third, *hollow*. Hollow. Why has he written hollow? How can that possibly fit into the context of the accident? Road damage — a Pete sized sinkhole? His life? My head? Perhaps it's best not to know any of what he's writing. I lean back in my chair and look at the wall above the filing cabinets. Since I was last here someone has stuck up a full colour poster-map of the world, which seems ridiculously out of place, a tongue-in-cheek reminder of what the team know they're missing out on, as they tramp from one shabby flat to the next.

I look back at Phil's hand just in time to see him write the last word, *action*. Then he makes an eccentric full stop. He drops the pen and looks up. 'How's the model coming along?'

'Not bad.'

'Do you think he's getting anything out of it?'

'I think so. But you know Pete. He doesn't really give much away.'

197

'How involved has he been?'

'He's had an input. But to be honest, I've done most of it so far.'

Phil nods slowly. 'There's definitely a place for taking the lead.' His voice is level now, calm, business-like. We are inside the sandwich. Not in the shit but definitely heading for it. 'There has to be some power in our role,' he goes on, 'otherwise rent would never get paid, shopping would never get done. But as you know, David,' — my ears prick up at the formal use of my name — 'it's about balance. I know I don't have to tell you this, but I will anyway.' There's an unfamiliar expression of seriousness on Phil's face now. 'You do good work with Pete,' he says. 'You seem to genuinely care about him, and that counts for a lot. But you do forget the small stuff now and again.' He pauses, inhales, exhales slowly. 'I know it's the hands-on stuff that really counts, but the paperwork's important too.

'I didn't fill in an incident report.'

'No, you didn't.' Phil deflates. His expression is almost apologetic. He's sorry to have reached the shit. He doesn't want to be saying any of this but knows he has to. 'And the thing is, David, they're pretty important.'

'I know.'

'How are your visit sheets looking? Are you

up to date with them?'

'I think there are two I have to write up from my notes.'

His eyes widen. Is he mocking or congratulating me? 'That's pretty good going,' he says, and his smile returns. 'Ray's about two weeks behind with his clients. All of them. But then he's been like that ever since he started here.' He pauses, seems to be considering a serious point. 'I mean what I say about the work you do with Pete. In some ways I think it's healthy for support workers to only work part time and have another passion. I think people like you bring something fresh to the job, another type of energy. You're probably the reason he made the drawings in the first place. An inspiration. And from what you've told me about them, they don't just sound like the scribbles of a lunatic.'

'No,' I say, 'they're pretty focused.' I sit up in my chair. 'Do you know what, Phil, if I'd walked into a London gallery and seen them, I'd have thought them the best work I'd come across in a long time.'

Phil takes a drag on his roll-up, then laughs, nodding. 'There is some rubbish out there though,' he says. 'Let's be honest.'

I nod in agreement. 'Believe me, I'm no defender of rubbish. I only go to see the odd show myself nowadays. Most of what's on doesn't appeal to me at all. Did you ever see the Prinzhorn collection at the Hayward? That was the last good show I saw. Art by inmates of German asylums.'

Phil takes hold of his chin and nods, but then smiles to let me know he's only half serious about it as a ponderous gesture. 'We have the catalogue somewhere,' he says. 'Some of it was amazing. Very detailed. At least there's some kind of talent in stuff like that — apart from the woman who'd scribbled all those joined up letter m's. They were pretty unsettling. There's a modern artist who does paintings a bit like that. Mary has a book about him.'

'Cy Twombly.'

'That's him.' Phil shakes his head, beaming. 'What a fantastic name.'

'I remember the scribbled m pieces,' I say. 'They were all called 'Letter to husband'.'

'I'm glad *I'm* not her husband.' Phil grimaces playfully and I have to laugh. I've now lost track of where we are in the sandwich. Phil has too. He leans back in his chair. 'Seriously though,' he says, 'with Pete's drawings, nothing you've told me sets any new alarm bells ringing, ones that we haven't already heard. There's obviously the concern about how focusing on the crash could impact on his emotional state, but as far as his mental health goes, you'd say he seems as stable as we can expect. Yes?'

I nod, then shrug. 'I don't know, Phil. How can you ever know with him? He's a bit of an enigma.'

Phil's roll-up has gone out, so he relights it. 'Look, David. The top and bottom of it is this. If he's going to kill himself, he will. He's tried before, and he was lucky. They were genuine attempts, not just cries for help. That wouldn't be Pete's style. I know that might sound cold, but that's how it is. I mean, eight Paracetamol can kill you for God's sake. There's so much out there that can. We just have to do what we can do, when we're there, on our visits. That's what you need to tell yourself. You can't do any more than that. The only thing I'd advise you to be careful with is how you continue to work with him creatively. Bear in mind that, inspired by you or not, he did make those drawings in his own time and through his own volition. And I know you said the model was his idea, but if I had a tenner for every time I've heard clients talk about things they intend to do, and then not follow through with them, well, I wouldn't be here on Walworth Road, that's for sure. Go easy. Let him set the pace. Our role here is to suggest alternatives to what the clients normally do, try to get them away from the TV, distract them from their day-to-day lives. But we do have to be careful about how forceful we are. They're very fragile. It's important to remember that. Simon once had a client, for example, a female client, and part of his work with her was to try to get her to clear out her junk mail. That was pretty much his remit. She'd allowed piles and piles of it to accumulate in her hall. I've never seen anything like it. There must have been ten years worth of it — pizza flyers, genuine mail to her, mail to ex-tenants, the lot of it covered in a fine layer of dust. He sat with her every morning, going through it all piece by piece, threw four bin liners of it away in seven weeks, thinking she was making good progress. Half way through the eighth week she was sectioned. She'd taken an overdose and phoned for an ambulance. The change was too much for her. It had all happened too fast.

'Ray has the same problem with Geoff Rowe. He's been seeing him for ten years now and they *still* haven't got round to clearing his spare room out. Geoff's just not up to it. Maybe he never will be. It's frustrating, I know, but we're not there to fast-track clients back to wellness, or challenge them. They've been challenged enough. I know you know all this stuff, David. But my job, unfortunately, is to remind you of it. That's what supervisions are.'

'I'd like to think I'm more encouraging than challenging him.'

'I'm sure you are. Fine line. Just take it easy. That's all I'm saying.'

I nod. 'Okay.'

'And like I said, if he is planning to kill himself, there's really not much you can do to stop him. What you *can* do is be careful not to push him into doing it sooner.'

I sigh. 'I know you're right, Phil. It's just frustrating to know that nothing can be done.'

Phil shrugs. 'It's a bit like terrorist attacks, David. If it's going to happen, it's going to happen. All you can do in the meantime is hope for the best.'

'I suppose so.'

'Excellent. Sorted.' Phil rubs his hands together again. 'Just one last thing. I think it's unlikely, but if the doctors make a connection between the haemorrhaging and the bus thing, well, we could have a bit of a problem on our hands.'

'But it happened outside visiting hours.'

'I know. It *was* connected with your model making though.'

'Which was his idea.'

'I know that too. I'm just saying that we

could do without an investigation into possible negligence. Nothing would stick, but we could just do without the hassle, all of us, including you — especially you.'

'I doubt they're connected.'

'Probably not.'

'Surely it would have happened anyway.'

'Lets hope so. How long will he be in hospital for?'

'They didn't say. I'm going over there later.'

'Good.' Phil picks up his pen again, and as he writes I look at the filing cabinet under the window where our Guidelines For Support Workers file is kept. What are my rights here? Do I have any? Am I insured? Are any of us? Could I go to prison if someone was injured or died in my care? And what's the procedure if it's discovered I'm withholding information about a family connection, not to mention knowledge of possible evidence relating to an arson attack? Maybe it would be wise to hang around later and do some reading up.

Phil stops writing and looks at me, and though I don't feel my expression is one of sadness, his kind smile suggests I could be wrong. 'I know you're having a tough time at the moment,' he says. 'I lost my dad five years ago and there are days when it still floors me. And you've got Sarah's sister ill as well. How's she doing, by the way?'

'She died last week.'

Phil shakes his head. 'Bloody hell, I'm sorry to hear that. You should have said something. You're going to need some more time off. When's the funeral?'

'Some time next week.'

'Well at least you don't have to worry about Pete. He's in safe hands. Hospital's probably the best place for him at the moment. This is just work, David. Family comes first. Always. I'll get Simon to cover you, if you need him to.'

I look Phil straight in the eye. Family comes first. The urge to tell him what he obviously doesn't know is suddenly overwhelming, but I manage to resist. Instead, and partly out of guilt for what feels like a betrayal of sorts, I earnestly say, 'If you ever leave this team, Phil, things will almost certainly fall apart.'

'Oh, don't think I don't know that,' he says. 'You lucky buggers have it good.' He grins. 'Write up that incident report before you leave and I'll backdate and file it.'

'Thanks,' I say. 'Did someone once help *you* out like this?'

'Of course they did. We are allowed to make *some* mistakes. None of us are perfect.' He tosses his pen down and narrows his eyes. 'Some of us are fairly close though, and I'll tell you, it can be a fucker of a burden.'

16

Pete remains unconscious through days three and four, and in his absence I begin to experience what can only be described as a form of guidance. Not spiritual — nothing like that — it's more like I can hear him taking me step by step through the creative process: Soak strips of newspaper in wallpaper paste and lay them down. No, not on the cardboard road — that needs to be completely flat. More paste . . . careful . . . watch out for lumps . . .

My own studio practice is very different. There, I work mostly on autopilot. Stretch canvas. Prime surface. Lay down background colour. Sketch out composition etc. My paintings arrive in the world via my hand and thoughts. They are mine and mine only. Collaboration is something new. I feel like a technician following orders.

After covering a quarter of the low-level wire frame, I realise what a mammoth task it will be to hide the chicken wire's hexagons. They still show through clearly, even after three layers.

I think for a while and make tea.

By lunchtime, after four more layers, the mountains are beginning to look fairly rock-like.

But then somehow it's Monday — day six — the weekend a kind of non-weekend (only one text from Sarah — *hope you're ok*) and I'm back again, tentative at first but quickly regaining confidence. Push here, dent there, I even poke a finger through the paper to pull the chicken wire back into shape (I can patch it up again later). At times I think there's a point to what I'm doing. Other times I feel stupid, ashamed even. I'm a childless, thirty-five year old man building a model in a garden shed.

After lunch I pour an inch of water into the lake. Then, down on my knees, I reach underneath the board to feel for leaks. Dry as a bone. Watertight. Nevertheless, I leave the water in there for a while, just to make sure.

Midafternoon and as I'm searching for more newspaper in the living room I come across a box of cigarette lighters in one of the alcove cupboards. An impressive collection. The police would have a field day. Lighters from different countries — Spain, Italy, Poland, Greece. Lighters from businesses — *FAIZ Quality Meat and Fish; Union cars*; **Double Tree Hotel; CHAL'S Mini-cabs**. Lighters with brand names printed on them — Electrolux, Canon, Zanussi, Marlboro. Lighters from supermarkets, bars, clubs, a music shop — even one from a launderette. I don't bother to count them, but at a glance

I take a guess at 150, maybe 200. I pick out two of the best. The orange and white clownfish (the head flips off, and when you press the fin to one side the flame clicks on) and the Spanish flamenco dancer attached to a dance floor ashtray (when you bend her forwards her skirt flips up and the flame shoots out from between her legs). Racy. I put them back in the box, the box back in the cupboard, feeling tired and certain about one thing: it's only a matter of time before he's taken in and questioned.

I decide not to go back to the shed for three days. Instead I do my own life.

Day seven: Paint and read.

Day eight: Cycle.

Day nine: Clare's funeral.

Halfway through the first hymn, I find it suddenly difficult to find a comfortable standing position. I rock from foot to foot, my hands clasped in front of my groin. Shivering, I study the ceiling, the huge plaster arches. I'm entirely surrounded by concrete and stone. The wood of the pews smells sweet. I watch, feeling numb, as the bearers bring in the coffin and place it on two wooden tressles. I picture the model on its tressles in the dark shed. Everything seems connected in some way, converging like the sides of a road as it disappears into the distance. Am I heading for a breakdown? It would be a lie to say I haven't thought about it recently. After all, mental illness runs in the family. I probably have a predisposition for it. Me and life are two tectonic plates. I am Eurasia. Life is North America. For thirty-five years we've pushed up against each other, and I've used mainly willpower and determination to get as far as I have. Life has been accommodating, flexible, but it has its limits. Sooner or later it will flip up and cast a permanent shadow over me.

I stare at the coffin, trying not to let my thoughts run away with me. I notice that Sarah is looking straight ahead. She's more discerning.

I feel nothing as an uncle reads Revelations 21:1–6. But when Sarah's mother gets to the second line of *Remember me*, and the first two syllables explode from her mouth, I notice that my throat tightens and my face twists. I look around for a distraction. Anything. I look beyond the priest at the small stained glass window. The image calms me, brings me back to some kind of centre. John is baptising Jesus in the river Jordan. The colours feel warm on my face. I think about Pete staring up at Jesus' shifting mosaic face, already knowing that he was going to kill himself on Christmas Day.

More singing. More prayers. We drive to the crematorium, then back to the church. We eat sandwiches and cakes and drink strong tea. After ten or fifteen minutes Sarah suggests we take a walk along the river. (She's probably struggling surrounded by all those cakes and biscuits.)

We make for the place we used to go to when we first met — a jetty next to a pub. As soon as we sit down, Sarah looks me in the eyes and says she misses me.

I respond appropriately. People lie at funerals all the time.

The next day I go to the park and read newspapers, the second half of a Paul Auster novel, and the first two chapters of a biography of Howard Hughes. That night, sitting on the boat's deck, watching people dance in the hotel bar opposite, I find myself thinking about certain events from childhood that were probably related to Pete's existence in the world. Dad howling in the night, crouched by the fireplace and hitting himself on the bridge of the nose with a small ornamental brass hammer (explanation: sinus headache); him coming home from the pub and picking arguments with my mother who'd long since been in bed (booze talking); her going AWOL for two weeks when I was eleven, three months when I was thirteen, and ten days when I was fifteen (no explanation ever offered); on her return, whole weekends spent in bed behind closed doors (migraine).

★ ★ ★

Day ten.

I paint the mountains with white under-coat, so that the greens and grey-blues I'll add later will glow, seemingly from within. I pick up my phone and make sure I have a signal. The hospital could call at any time.

There you go.

When I arrive on the ward he's packed and ready, sitting on the edge of the bed, his cast leg propped up on an orange plastic chair. The small white paper bag he's clutching contains a small bottle of Co-Dydramol, some Chlormethiazole, and Heminevrin for the symptoms of alcohol withdrawal.

All week long I've spoken to nurses only, and they've repeated the same old thing — haemorrhage, haemorrhage, haemorrhage. A doctor is available now, but he seems cagey at first. I explain that I'm aware about disclosure of information but then stress that since I'm the person who's around most of the time, it surely makes sense to advise me on how to best take care of him.

'What made him lose consciousness is some-thing called Varices,' the doctor says. 'Some patients have varicose veins which pour into the oesophagus. If these rupture and bleed into the oesophagus, the patient is in effect given a high-dosage protein meal. If this happens to someone with a healthy liver, the body is able to cope with the amount of protein. If, on the other hand, the liver is damaged, as it is in Mr Doran's case, extensively, then the body can't cope with the protein and the person loses consciousness and can easily die. We were lucky to have been able to stop the bleeding at all. Sometimes we can't.'

'And if the same thing happens again?'

'There isn't really much you can do, other than call for an ambulance.' At this point the doctor looks down at Pete. 'And as for you, fresh air, rest, take the Heminevrin for five days, and don't drink.'

★   ★   ★

When we get home we fill the lake together. Thirty pints. We add a tablespoon of Spirulina powder to turn the water green and stand back to take a look. It's an odd scene — winter meets summer, plush green lowlands surrounded by snow-white mountains — but there's still a lot to do.

We sort through the branches I gathered together while Pete was in hospital. Holding them at arms length, we try to picture them as trees. We put the most convincing ones to the side and throw the rest in the garden.

Next, we pulp up more of the modroc and place small balls of it here and there. I let Pete stick the trees in the balls. Then I show him how to blend the trunks to the base.

'I need to go soon,' I tell him. 'I'll take the Mini back to the boat and assemble it over the weekend.'

He hands me a key. 'Here. I got a set cut for you. It probably makes sense for you to have one.'

★ ★ ★

Day eleven.

Tamiya Mini Cooper 1275S Mk 1

Tools needed: a sharp knife, a small screwdriver, a file, and a pair of thin-nosed pliers.

Colours: Flat White. Green. Orange. Red. Lemon Yellow. Gun Metal. Semi Gloss Black. Flat Black. Clear Red. Hull Red. Flat Green. Flat Aluminium. Sky Grey. Medium Grey. Metallic Grey. Red Brown. Chrome Silver.

I look at the instructions, read some of the history but take none of it in. I remove the plastic bags and examine the parts. A small see-through bag contains four rubber tyres. I study them from different angles. They have tread. They look like liquorice. DUNLOP

213

RADIAL SP3 is written around the walls in tiny capitals.

I go up on deck and lay out a sheet of newspaper. If a breeze gets up I may have to go back down below, otherwise the parts could blow away and end up in the water. What will Sarah be doing now? Powering up and down the pool? And Faye? She's probably more of a paddler, a lilo lounger. What is it that I find so attractive about her? Apart from the fact that she has a great figure, dark eyes, a nice voice and smile, what exactly is it? That she's a mother? That's definitely part of it. Unlike my mother, she made sacrifices, gave up what she was doing to bring up a baby.

I pop off the lids of the enamel paints — Flat Green, Flat Aluminium, Semi Gloss Black, and Metallic Grey. These are the colours for the engine parts. Using the 00 brush, I paint them.

An hour later, the parts are dry enough to handle. I snip them away from the sprue, filing away the excess plastic and touching them up again where they need it. I've now mastered the needlepoint glue applicator. How not to squeeze too hard. How to judge the subtle delay between the squeeze and the appearance of the tiny bead of glue on the tip of the nozzle. By lunchtime the painted

214

engine is attached to the subframe. By midafternoon I've painted, snipped, filed and repainted my way through stage 3 (assemblage of front brakes); 4 (attaching front brakes); and 5 (attaching the engine). I assemble the rear suspension and attach the wheels. Stage 9 next: attaching seat rail; 10: dashboard and seats; 11: carburettor; 12: body and windows.

I go down below, slice up a pineapple and eat it standing up, juice dripping down my chin. I make a strong coffee and go out on deck again to watch the waitresses lay tables outside the front of the harbour hotel. I finish only half the coffee because it makes me feel jittery. A steady hand is essential when using a 00 brush.

Then it's back down below again to paint the body Flat White. I clip the glass of the headlights into the small casings, which I've already painted Chrome Silver. I click the radiator grill in place and glue the front and rear bumpers to the body. I fill a saucer with water, cut up the transfers and soak them for twenty seconds. I slide them off the paper and apply.

Done.

I'm woken some time in the night by the mooring ropes stuttering out creaks. I reach for the notepad I keep by the bed in case I have a good idea. *Happy Accident*, my painting of the blind accordion player stumbling his way out of the felled forest, will be re-titled *Can't See the Wood For the Trees*.

★   ★   ★

On Monday morning, day twelve, back in the shed, it takes around fifteen minutes to paint the mountains with the first coat of blue-grey. When the paint is dry I use a sponge scourer to create patches of earthy looking brown and black. I partly sand the paint off in areas (for that weather-beaten look). On the lower level areas, I create the effect of scree by painting on PVA and scattering on fine gravel. By four o'clock, satisfied with the mountains, I paint the green areas around the lake.

After only the first coat, the whole thing really seems to be coming together. Later, when I show Pete how to add darker shades of green, to give weight to the dips, and lighter greens for where sunlight catches the rises, what we'll have in front of us could be far better than we imagined.

An hour later I trim six inches of Pete's cast away, so that he can bend his leg without the sharp edge of the fibreglass digging into the back of his knee. While he's off boiling the kettle, I move around the model sowing green and brown scatter material onto damp paint, smiling to myself about the fake weather he's left behind — blue cigarette smoke that shifts and swirls, or just hangs low like morning mist. I spray a cloud of Spraymount over the mountains and sprinkle on a few more handfuls of grey scatter material.

Clare is grey powder in a bag inside a box on its way to South Africa. Her parents will find a beach and cast handful after handful of her into the sea. Did Sarah go with them or stay behind?

I go back to the harbour and sit up on deck to watch the sun set behind the hotel.

Later, down below, under dim lights that are almost certainly damaging my eyes, I make a dry-stone wall out of card. It takes almost an hour to paint it, and it doesn't turn out well. Instinct tells me that it won't look right, won't sit right — and the next day, day thirteen, back in the shed, I find that my instinct *was* right. No matter how I position it along the edge of the unfinished road, it rises up slightly at one end, refuses to look solid or heavy, even when I half close my eyes and step back.

It's no use. I crumple it up and throw it in the bin. It's the first failure but by no means the end of the world.

I cover the slip road and car park with

PVA. Pete mixes some light brown and Tarmac scatter material together. When we're happy with the colour, convinced, until we believe in it, we sprinkle it on carefully and blow off the excess.

I lay newspaper over the slip road to protect it. I cut out thin strips of paper for the main road's white lines. They need to be slightly raised from the surface so that once we sprinkle on the black Tarmac powder they'll be level with it, flush. I round off the corners slightly; I don't want them to look too angular — that's not how white lines are. I paint the whole of the road area with PVA mixed with black paint and press the white lines into place. Using a flour sieve, we scatter on the Tarmac powder and Hoover off the excess. I paint the white lines gloss white. Then I position the car and camper van a few millimetres apart, the split second before impact.

Thirteen days. Not bad. It's over.

We stand back to take a look. Pete turns to face me. 'It's Llanberis,' he says. 'North Wales. I remember now. It just came to me.'

17

The tedium of our mornings has returned. The model now finished, we have resorted to watching reruns of reruns of *Supernanny*.

Two children — a four year old boy and six year old girl — won't stay in their beds and are screaming from the top of the stairs like wild animals. The dad has tried to settle them eight times, each time under strict instruction not to exchange words. He goes for ninth time lucky but only makes it halfway down the stairs before the boy appears on the landing, the beginnings of a sob already in his throat. Dad turns around and trudges back up towards him. He's a patient man. I have no idea what I'd do in his position.

Over the last two days I've regularly gone out to the shed to admire the model. It really is impressive, somehow far more meaningful than painting. A couple of times I actually felt myself welling up.

Music is apparently at the top of the list, art form wise, for making people cry. Then Film. Then Novels. Then Painting. Modroc and plastic cars, though? Who would have thought it?

Pete has showed no further interest. For him, once something is finished, he draws a line under it. Full stop.

It's all too much. I can't watch another second. Time-lapse video has just informed us that Dad is about to attempt bedtime #15.

I get to my feet. 'It's a four hour drive to North Wales. We could go. If Sarah hasn't gone to South Africa I'm sure she'll lend us her car.'

'Why would she do that, after everything that's happened?'

'Because she's not precious about her stuff. Besides, she hardly uses it. I'll phone her.'

It turns out I'm right, she hasn't gone with her parents, and she says we can take the car for as long as we like.

Pete and I agree on a two-day trip, and we'll leave as soon as possible.

I spend the rest of the morning in the internet café around the corner looking for somewhere to stay. We'll also need a map, a real map, so after lunch I cycle over to Stanfords in Covent Garden.

The shop is on two levels.

Maps are in the basement.

I head downstairs and approach a man who's holding a stack of files against his chest. 'Excuse me,' I say. 'Can you help me? I'm an artist working on a project about memory. My brother drew a map of a place but he can no longer remember where it is. He's narrowed it down to a small-ish area, but we need to find the exact spot. What would you do? Just buy an OS map of the area and look for similar matches?'

'I suppose so. Do you have anything specific to go on?'

'It's near Lanberis.'

'You could look in the Gazetteer.'

'What's that?'

'I'll show you.'

I follow him over to a large desk with a glass top. He puts the stack of files down and opens a huge, leather bound tome. 'This will give you a reference. Near Lanberis you say. What was the name of the village?'

'We don't know.'

'Oh, okay, well then your best bet is the most detailed OS map of Snowdonia. If you want a very small area we have a digital department and they can print off large-scale maps. For £20 you get a highly detailed square kilometre.'

'I thought there might be a computer programme that would find matches for you, if you scanned in the details of a place. Some kind of GPS thing.'

'Worded information?'

'No, just lines. A sketch. Topography.'

'I don't know of anything like that.'

'It's a strange query, I suppose.'

'You need a hard reference. If you have that, you can find any place on the planet. You could always look on Google Earth, but a map's actually better.'

'Really? That surprises me. Which OS series do I need? Orange or pink?'

'Pink.'

'Pink it is.'

★　★　★

I'm back at Pete's but he doesn't appear to be around. Filling the kettle I look towards the shed, but the door is padlocked and the light off. I take out a cup and find we're out of teabags. I open out the OS map, lay it on the table and quickly mark red boxes around sections of road that are similar in shape to the section in the model. It's not an exact science, but it's the only way I can think of.

Five minutes later, back from the corner shop and sipping tea on the kitchen doorstep, I hear faint sobbing. I look over towards the shed and notice that the padlock is now no longer on the door — though it is still closed. I creep across the garden and peer in through the window. Pete's rolled up close to the model, his head hanging forwards, his shoulders shaking. He's separated the car and camper van and placed them on their respective sides of the road. If they were to move now they'd pass each other without incident. For the first time since finding out we're flesh and blood I feel genuine brotherly love for him.

I pull open the door and he looks my way. Tears are streaming down his face and he makes no attempt to hide them.

'I made tea,' I say.

He shakes his head. 'Tea isn't the answer to everything. Have *you* done much of this?'

'What?'

'Crying.'

'Not lots.'

'You need to. It will get you in the end. Just because she lied to you all that time, doesn't mean her death won't knock you for six. A panic attack isn't grief. That's just the tip of the iceberg. I'll give you a bit of advice. If you ever decide to let go, don't do it with both hands. That's what I did, years ago, and look at me.'

★   ★   ★

An hour later I'm washing dishes when the doorbell goes.

It turns out to be Faye.

Today she's wearing a khaki shirt, denim skirt, black shiny boots and the same earrings she was wearing the day she let me use the phone — small silver loops with dangling green beads. Her hair, though, is different again. This time it's woven into thin, tight, scalp hugging braids. 'Hi,' she says. She recoils slightly. 'Are you okay?'

'I'm fine. Just tired.'

'I saw the ambulance the other day. Is Mr Doran ill?'

'He has been. He was in hospital for a while, but he's back home now.'

'Good. How are you getting on with your model? Did you make it?'

I nod. 'Do you want to see it?'

'I can't. Little man's asleep. I just ran out to get some pepper. Some other time though. Definitely.'

'Your hair suits you. It must have taken a long time.'

'Eight hours.'

'Eight hours?'

'I have a lot of patience. I have to, I'm a single mum.'

There's a nervous silence.

'I'm glad you called round,' I say. 'I'm going away for a few days. But when I get back, do you fancy meeting up for a coffee?'

She nods. 'Or food?'

'Okay, great.'

'I love food. What's your favourite dish?'

'Lasagne. You?'

'Indian,' she says. 'And some Caribbean. I love Yam.'

'I don't think I've ever had it.'

'It's lovely and filling. I love that full feeling.' She laughs at herself. 'Are you local?'

'At the moment I'm living on a boat in Chelsea Harbour.'

'Sounds romantic.'

'Not really. It's a long story.'

'Well, you can tell me about it when you get back, if you like. I could come over and visit you. I love boats. I haven't been on one in ages. Let me give you my number.'

I get out my phone and key it in.

★ ★ ★

Pete and I have cooked dinner together, and for the first time since I've known him, it didn't seem like work. We actually *felt* like brothers as we moved around the kitchen, instinctively stepping out of each others way, knowing when to talk and when not to. We've made our speciality — seafood pasta (prawns, mussels and squid in a crème frâiche and pesto sauce).

We sit down. Pete tucks in and polishes off

a fairly decent sized amount. By the time we've finished, though, a feeling of melancholy has come over me, and for some reason I can't help thinking about prisoners on death row eating their final meal.

I wash the dishes. Pete dries. At around 10 p.m., I help him into bed and tell him to be up bright and early.

On the way back to the boat I pass by home to collect the car key. There's a note taped to the front door: *Hi. Check your texts.*

I do and there's one from Sarah: *I'm out. Car key under recycling box. Hope you both find what you're looking for. Good luck. Take care. S. xx*

III

18

It's 9 a.m. and we are halfway along a huge lake on our left. Pete has slept for most of the journey and hardly spoke when he was awake. I slow down and pull into a narrow lay-by, running the passenger side wheels up onto a grass bank edged with yellow-flowered bushes. Sarah's Mini tilts to the right more than I expect, sending Pete toppling towards me. I push him back into his seat. He blinks repeatedly and as he's vigorously rubbing his cheeks, I point the Polaroid camera at him.

'Don't,' he says, wiping spittle from the sides of his mouth.

I click the button and the flash surprises me. The camera whirrs and the picture slides out. 'I'm not sure about the way from here,' I say. 'I'll have to take a look at the map.'

'Does she ever clean this car?' he says. 'Look at the state of it.' He points to the inset, the clocks. A collection of orange peelings and balls of chewing gum partly obscure the speedometer.

I reach into the back for the map. Under my green pullover I find the flask. 'Here.' I unfold the map on the steering wheel. Pete unscrews the thermos, its cup wedged between his thighs. 'Do you have any other cups?'

'I'm not sure. Maybe on the floor near your feet.'

He leans forwards and finds a white enamel one under some papers. 'You have the red one,' he says. 'I don't like drinking out of coloured cups, the tea never looks brewed.'

I soon work out where we are by studying the shape of the lake. We are just a few miles this side of Llanberis. I put on the wipers and peer up the road to see if I can see the turn off. The visibility isn't good — too much mist, the rain heavy again now, dark towers of it sweeping horizontally across the lake. There are far more red boxes on the map than I remember making. Visiting them all won't be easy.

'This could be one of the sites,' I say. 'And it's not even one of the ones I marked.'

Pete shakes his head dismissively. 'It couldn't. The lake's on the wrong side. And those houses over there are old. There *were* no houses nearby.'

I laugh. 'It wouldn't be on the wrong side if we were going the other way.'

He shrugs, unsmiling. 'No. I suppose not.'

I wind down the window. A short convoy of cars hisses by, rocking us. Once they've passed, the only sound is the rain on the roof and the wind rattling the aerial against it. Pete sips quietly at his tea, looking straight ahead at nothing in particular. Through his passenger side window I watch the blurred moving forms of a group of people in yellow waterproofs and matching helmets launching canoes on the far side of the lake. A wave of rain hits the left side of the car, the drops twitch on the window and turn the canoeists into wriggling blobs of colour. I lean across Pete's lap and rub at the condensation. He peers through the clear patch and shakes his head. 'Mad.'

'I agree. I wouldn't go out on the water on a day like this.' It's eerily quiet suddenly. I wind my window down an inch. 'I think it's easing off. What was the weather like on the day of the accident?'

'Sunny. Misty in the morning. Sunny when we crashed.'

★   ★   ★

After ten minutes the sky clears a little, and up ahead, where the lake narrows, the water suddenly seems blacker and less choppy. A patch of sun hits the mountainside, painting it bright orange.

'That rusty colour,' I say. 'We didn't add

any of it to the model.'

Pete takes a sip of his tea. 'Iron. It's like that because of all the iron in the rock.'

'I mean the bracken.'

'Can you turn the wipers off? That squeaking's driving me mad.'

I do as he says. Then I pull the Polaroid from the camera. The image has now fully developed, and seeing him frozen like that, his cheeks sunken, his mouth gaping, it suddenly strikes me that he really isn't a well man. The flash has bleached him, penetrated his thin skin to reveal the lurking sickness beneath it. The sockets of his eyes are dark, the shadows under his cheekbones pro-nounced. He looks like the head in Munch's *The Scream*. I pass the picture to him. He takes a quick look and throws it on the floor.

We sit watching the rain thin, and by the time we've emptied the thermos, it's stopped altogether. I wind down my window fully. The air smells very clean. There are no bird sounds. No sounds at all in fact. It feels good to be here, away from the city. My thoughts seem clearer, more purposeful.

Cascading down the hillside on our right is a fast flowing river that forms a small but powerful waterfall in the gap between two lengths of dry-stone wall. Pete squints. 'That water looks like snow,' he says. 'Powder, not liquid. Dry not wet. It's the whiteness of the white. Are you seeing that too?'

'Sort of,' I say. 'White isn't a colour.'

'It's made up out of all the other colours. White light.'

'Yes,' I say. 'The spectrum.'

'The colour wheel.'

'I can't remember exactly what that is. I should, but I don't.'

'It's what it says. A wheel of all the colours. Primary and secondary. Black isn't a colour either.'

'No,' I say. 'No light.'

He arranges the sleeping bag against the window and plumps it. 'I need some more sleep. How much further?'

'About two miles.'

'Wake me up when we get there.'

I start the engine and pull away.

We hiss through water that spills from the steep banks and sends spray into hedges and onto the trunks of trees. After a few miles we hit mist again, and everything vanishes but the white lines. We stop to let four sheep cross the road. One lingers, looks at us, and it's only when I edge forward and almost touch it that it decides to trot off and join the others.

After a few hundred yards I spot a trailer in front of us loaded up with long logs, the rough-sawn ends pointing back at us.

Balancing on top of the load is a large wooden wheel — a mill wheel possibly — which is roped on but looks far from secure. We sweep left around a long bend and the load leans precariously to the right. More mist. A sign reading GWYNEDD looms up, followed by one for LLANBERIS. The trailer indicates right. I follow it and we begin our climb.

'I hope those logs don't fall off,' Pete says. 'Are your lights on?'

I brush the orange peelings aside and check the dashboard. 'Yes.'

We pass another sign — a black sheep in a red triangle — that someone has spray-painted EVIL FARMERS onto in green, angular capitals.

Pete shakes his head. 'We shouldn't have come here.'

'Amazing view,' I say. I gesture to the left. 'If it was a clearer day you'd be able to see Snowdon. It's over there somewhere.'

The climb steepens. Peaks and horizon lines disappear and re-emerge from slowly drifting clouds. I take the car down into second gear. On our left is a low dry-stone wall that in some places is so damaged it's little more than two or three stones balanced on top of each other. On the other side of it I can sense the drop, feel the empty space behind the whiteness. The mist thins, moves quickly, and in a matter of seconds it's cleared completely, as though it's been sucked up by a giant vacuum cleaner. The valley appears before us. Sharp. Vivid. My heart swells. Even Pete seems impressed. Deep greens and greys rise on both sides. Ahead, where the land flattens, a pine forest and a huge rectangular lake stretch out before us.

Pete re-scrunches the upper folds of the sleeping bag against the window, leans into it and closes his eyes.

I shake my head in disbelief. 'How can you sleep with views like this? We're on top of the world here. This road can't have changed at all over the last forty years. There's not really much you *can* change when you have a sheer drop on one side and a mountain on the other.'

'No.'

Around the next bend the road straightens and rises to a collection of stone buildings that appear to mark the top of the climb. As we get closer I see a sign: CAR PARK FULL. I slow down. On our left, around most of the cars, groups of people are dressing for a day's walking. Along a path that begins at a gate in the corner of the car park, a stream of brightly coloured jackets moves steadily towards the mountain.

A white VW Camper is waiting in the middle of the road, its right indicator blinking. I flash my lights. Pete looks up to see why we've stopped, and when he sees the Camper he does a classic double take. He glances at me, then back at the Camper again — as though it's some supernatural manifestation I'm responsible for.

Seen from above we must look almost exactly like the model.

The Camper's driver, a man in his sixties, waves a thank you and turns into the car park. The moment of eerie significance passes.

I pull away and we began to drop into the valley.

The scree is much darker than in the model, possibly because it's wet. Apart from such minor details we did a fairly good job.

We continue our descent and after a while, the road levels out. We pass a series of small passing bays, most of which are full of parked cars. When we see a bus stop Pete laughs out loud. 'Imagine waiting there for a bus.'

'I'd rather wait there than on Walworth road.'

The field we are passing on our left, the back third rising halfway up the hills, is dotted with brightly coloured tents, towels flapping from guy ropes.

We enter a small village. Five or six houses and a pub. The high mountains are behind us now. Here there are only hills. A mile or so further on we begin to pass the huge lake we could see from higher up. On its far side are the disused slate quarries I remember noticing on the map. The whole side of the face is a blue-grey mass of dots, cracks, and zigzagging pale green and yellow paths. We sweep around a series of bends until up ahead I spot a small castle on top of a grassy knoll.

'We're here,' I say, as a sign saying CROESO-LLANBERIS slips by.

Pete opens his eyes and stretches his neck. His head swivels and jerks, bird-like.

'Even the road markings are in Welsh. Araf must mean slow.'

Ignoring me, he leans forward and narrows his eyes at a large white hotel up ahead. 'What about there,' he says. 'That place looks nice. Better than the place we're staying at, I bet. Buffalo Bill's.'

'It's called Jesse James', and I think that place would be a bit out of our price range.'

'Jesse James',' he says under his breath. 'What is a bunkhouse, anyway?'

'It's like a youth hostel, but smaller.'

'I bet it's full of these lot.' He points out a couple in matching purple waterproofs who are waiting at a zebra crossing up ahead, just before a left turn into what looks like the village. I stop to let the couple cross. The man raises his hand to thank us.

In the village Spar I buy milk, bread, tea bags, bananas, chocolate, and some tobacco for Pete (he prefers roll-ups on holiday). Back in the car, I pass the carrier bag to him. He looks inside and moves the contents around. 'No apples?' He chuckles to himself. 'You could have at least got me some cans.'

'We can find a pub this evening.'

'I don't go to pubs in the evenings. I only go in the afternoon.'

'A change of routine will do you good.'

We drive for a hundred yards or so and I spot a café called PETE'S EATS, which I find so comical I pull over outside. 'Are you hungry?'

'Let's see this place of yours first.'

★ ★ ★

About two miles out of the village I spot the turn off that will take us to the bunkhouse. Blocking it, though, is a truck with a large sign on the back: SLOW! ROAD MARKING IN PROGRESS. I pull up and we watch the men work. Pete seems fascinated by the process. One man pours liquid tar from a bucket into the square holes cut out for the cat's eyes. Behind him, another man waits a few seconds before placing the cat's eyes down. Another two men are marking white arrows on the road, one holding a sheet metal template in position while the other pushes a wheelbarrow/paint roller hybrid over the arrow-shaped cut-out. Thick white smoke rises up around them. There's something vaguely menacing about the scene.

'I wonder how they get the white paint to dry so quickly,' Pete says. 'Look, cars are already driving over it and it's not smudging.'

The men wave us towards them and we head up the hill.

Pete checks in the mirror. 'See. No smudges.'

And after what seems much more than 100m, there it is: The Jesse James Bunkhouse. A pale yellow building with red wooden flashing. I park on the small gravel car park next to two upside down catamarans.

I get out for a stretch. Then, following a cardboard sign that says **OFFICE** I walk around the side of the house. The 'office' is actually the kitchen, and although there's a felt-tip-on-paper **ENTER** sign taped to the inside of the window, I knock and wait. No-one comes. I knock again. Still nothing. I open the door. 'Hello?' No answer. I walk back around to the car and find Pete smoking, his cast sticking out through the open passenger side door.

'I can't find anyone.'

He looks up at me. 'Did you book?'

'Yes.'

Rustling in the trees, some movement among the branches, and a tall old man in overalls and a matching baseball cap emerges. Moving quickly for someone his age, he strides towards us waving a green handled hammer as a friendly greeting. Pete drops his cigarette and toes it into the gravel. Smokers aren't welcome here. He's sensed that somehow.

'Jesse?' I say.

The old man crunches to a stop and holds out his free hand. 'Hello there,' he says.

I shake his hand. 'I have a room booked. Under Price.'

'David,' he says as though we are old friends. 'Under price? We're already cheap as it is.' He laughs. There are dried patches of tomato soup or sauce at the corners of his mouth. 'Sorry. I bet you've heard that one before, eh?'

I smile politely. 'It's not the first time.'

'So,' he says. 'All the way from London. City slickers. I've given you Castle of the Winds. It's around the back.' He holds the hammer horizontally between us, as though it's a scroll he's presenting, our reward for having made the journey here. The lime green handle is reflected and multiplied in his glasses. 'If you go around the side there, you'll hear a Hoover going upstairs. That's Maggie. She should be getting things ready for you. I'm just on my way out. You're lucky to have caught me.' He points at a gap in the hedge where a neat looking shed stands next to a rectangle of brick bordered concrete. 'I've just moved that,' he says. 'Less 'in your face' over there. Doesn't jump out at you when you come from around the back of the building. I'm going to turn that foundation into a patio for barbecues. Build one of those chimney affairs you see in Greek tavernas. It'll be lovely on those balmy summer evenings. You know, the two we get per year.' He chuckles. 'We'll be able to sit out. A strum on the old guitar. A scratch of the navel while we stargaze. Wait till you see the stars here. Take no notice of the clouds. We could easily get a clear night tonight.'

Pete coughs behind me and Jesse steps to the side. 'Hello there.'

'Hello,' Pete says.

'Shall I pay you now or later?' I ask.

Jesse throws up his hand. 'Oh don't worry about all that. Bloody money. Nothing but trouble. Sort it out with Maggie. I'll be gone for a couple of days but she'll look after you.

Have a good time. Enjoy the mountains, but respect them.'

'I don't think we'll be going up there.'

'No? You should at least go up to the slate mines. There are old miners' dormitories up there. Coats still hanging on hangers. Boots under the benches. You can smell the history up there, almost hear the tools chipping away.'

'I doubt I'll get him up there in a wheelchair.'

'It's not steep. And there's a decent path. You could easily push him up, a fit young man like you. I still go up, and look at me. Or you could take him up to the top of Snowdon on the train. It goes right to the summit. Get yourselves a cuppa at the café up there.'

I laugh.

'I'm serious,' he says. 'There's one up there. They've just refurbished it. It's like a bloody motorway service station. They've spoiled that mountain something terrible. A train up a mountain. I ask you. You get all kinds up there now. People in jeans even.'

★ ★ ★

The staircase to Castle of the Winds is rickety and narrow, more a semi-permanent ladder. It's a struggle carrying Pete up. His feet catch on the banister. His cast scrapes and bumps against the tongue-and-groove wall. A woman with long grey, tied back hair switches off the Hoover when she sees our heads appear in the room. She straightens up and girlishly flicks her fringe from her eyes.

'Hi,' I say.

'Hello, I'm Maggie.' She points at her chest as though using some form of sign language.

'I'm David.'

She smiles. 'And you must be Peter.'

Pete nods. 'Pete.'

I carry him over to the window and set him down on an orange patchwork sofa. His face lights up when he sees the TV. He looks at Maggie. 'Do you have Sky?'

'No, I'm afraid not. Besides, I'm sure you haven't come here to watch television.'

'No,' I say. 'We haven't.'

Maggie nods. 'I'll leave you to it then. A few things though, before I do.' She walks over to the window and all three of us look outside. The long grass and tall trees lean in the wind, then come back to centre again. Maggie places her palm on top of an electric storage heater. 'This little thing really puts out some heat. It can sometimes get chilly in here, but if you put this on, say an hour before you go to bed, you should be fine. We ask people not to leave it on all night because it does run up quite a bill. If you do forget, and people sometimes do, we only charge 8p per unit.' She walks briskly past me into the kitchen area — a small round sink, a toaster, and a two ring camping stove connected to a butane bottle.

'Is there a kettle?' I ask.

'Oh yes, I think we bought a new one for this room. The old one blew up. It's probably still in the house. I'll get it in a minute.' She opens the fridge — empty apart from a half full plastic bottle of milk. She takes it out, opens it and sniffs. 'Someone left this. It's still okay. Do you want it?'

'Thanks,' I say.

'We don't allow smoking inside. We usually ask people to go outside.' She smiles at Pete. 'I know in your case that's not easy. I'm sorry but that's the rule. Too much wood you see.'

'Yes,' I say. 'There is a lot.'

She nods. 'We like wood.'

'How do you know I'm a smoker?' Pete asks.

'Aren't you?'

'Yes.'

Maggie grins. 'I don't miss much. I'm good at spotting types.' She winks at me. 'Come with me. I'll find that kettle.'

I follow her down the stairs, she goes in the house, and when she comes out with the

244

kettle she's also carrying two clean red and white checked tea towels. 'Leave the key under the dustbin whenever you go out,' she says. 'We always ask people to get into the habit of doing that. The ones that don't sometimes end up going all the way home with the keys, and then they have to post them back to us.' She hands me the kettle and tea towels.

'It's a great place you have here.'

'We like it.'

Back in the room I put the kettle on, and as it's boiling I lift Pete up onto the wide pine windowsill. I open the window and he sits there smoking, the orange blanket draped around his shoulders like a poncho. He blows smoke out into the wind. It darts to the left but some drifts back in the room.

'She'll know,' I say.

★　★　★

Maggie is hanging washing out on a line that wasn't up when we arrived. I have to stoop under it to get to the car.

'Hi,' she says when she sees me. 'No rest for the wicked.'

I watch her peg up a duvet cover and matching pillowcases, a white under-sheet, and a black lace bra. She seems younger than she did up in the room. She catches me looking and smiles.

Our bags upstairs, I come down again to look for a place to store the wheelchair. I find a small, musty smelling cupboard, empty apart from a pair of walking boots and a stack of newspapers, and I fold the chair and put it in there.

I check the car is locked, and as I'm heading back towards the house I feel a few drops of rain. I walk over to the living room window and see Maggie vacuuming again. I knock but she doesn't hear me. I knock again and she glances up. She hurries over to the switch and cuts the power. Then she walks towards me and opens the window.

I gesture towards the washing. 'It's spitting.'

'Oh,' she says, unfazed. 'I'll come out. Thank you.'

By the time she comes striding across the lawn, wearing round sunglasses with yellow lenses, a sheet is draped over my shoulder, a pillowcase over my forearm.

'Thanks again,' she says, unpegging a towel. 'Is your friend going to be okay?'

'He's fine.'

'He doesn't look well.'

'He'll be okay. Jesse's quite a character.'

She laughs. 'He's deaf sometimes, when he

wants to be. Selective hearing. I bet he didn't make you pay. He hates talking about money. That's what I liked about him when we met. It's a miracle we manage to keep this place open.'

★ · ★ · ★

Just after 11 a.m., I drive us down into the village and park outside PETE'S EATS. I unfold the wheelchair and help Pete into it. A woman holds the café door open. The man she's with helps me lift the chair up the step.

Walkers are huddled over plates of food and steaming drinks. The walls are covered in the same tongue and groove boarding as our room in the bunkhouse, but here it's been stained green. Photographs of climbers are everywhere, some framed, most simply fixed up with Blu-tack. Next to the counter is an OS map of the Himalayas.

I order two large teas, scrambled eggs on brown toast, and white toast for Pete. The woman serving gives me a pink ticket and tells me to listen out for my number.

I push Pete through the large room and we cause quite a stir. Almost half the café has to stand to create a walkway for us to some free seats by the window.

'No smoking?' Pete asks.

'You know there isn't.'

On the wall opposite the counter is a large collage of photographs of people engaged in action sports. In one, a man is leaping across two dark peaks that appear to be hundreds of feet up. The evening sun glows between his spread legs.

When our food arrives I start on the eggs. Pete plays around with the toast, taking only the occasional nibble (not unlike Sarah, but for some reason it doesn't irritate me in the same way).

Two men in fleeces and woolly hats come and take the seats to our right, and the one who sits diagonally across from me — long blonde hair, ruddy face — begins talking about a girl called Moonie. 'She can do most of the climbs in Chamonix with her eyes closed,' he says.

The other man shakes his head. 'Fucking nutter. Have you seen Wombat lately?'

'Nah. Not since The Three Peaks Challenge.'

'How did he get on?'

'Collapsed halfway up Scafell. Dehydration and low carb intake.'

Pete raises his eyes. 'I'm ready to go when you are.'

I gesture at his plate. 'Eat a bit more.'

He shakes his head. 'I'm not hungry. You finish it.'

Half an hour later we are parked up in a lay-by. Site 1. On our right is a lake, up ahead, on the left, another lay-by. Fifty yards in front of us is the modern-looking Lake View Hotel. Beyond that I can see a blind left hand bend.

'Imagine the hotel isn't there,' I say. 'What do you think?'

'It all looks the same here. We'll never find it.'

I get out of the car, take a Polaroid, get back in and pull away. As we creep past the hotel, Pete studies the image as it fades up.

'Mark it number one,' I say. 'There's a felt pen on the floor. I numbered the sites on the map before we left. They should correspond.'

He writes a small 1 in the top left hand corner of the Polaroid and pops the top back on the pen. We head into the blind bend and he looks over to the right. 'There's no slip road anyway,' he says. He points at the lake that stretches out for about another mile up ahead. 'The water ended about here. Just before the bend. The slip road went down over there to a car park.'

I accelerate.

'Not so fast.'

I ease off.

At the second site it's pretty much the same thing. Again the bend is right, and the natural features are evidence enough that the road's shape couldn't have changed much over the years. This time, though, what troubles Pete is a small church on the steep slope to our right, just back from the bend. A short slip road next to it appears to lead around the back. There's also a small car park, enough space for six or seven cars. Rising up behind is a plantation of fir trees.

'How old do you think those are?' I say.

'I've no idea.'

I get out and take a Polaroid of the slip road.

'That's a waste of a picture,' he shouts. 'There was definitely no church.'

By midafternoon we've clocked up more than sixty miles and are at site number seven, drinking stewed tea in yet another lay-by. My map reading skills have surprised me. With most of the matches I chose there have only been one or two problems — road too narrow or too wide; too many buildings; lake too small or wrong shape; no slip road (or slip road too straight); no car park; mountains too high — but I'm beginning not to care. I'm enjoying being on the road surrounded by open space. My shoulders and neck have loosened up. I've even felt a surprising urge to paint landscapes (maybe I should invest in a smock and beret). The mountains in front of us are so sharp, so in-focus, it feels as though I could reach out and touch them.

'We're not far from a village called Beddgelert,' I say. 'I read about it in a leaflet at Jesse's. We could drive there and have a look round, take a break. It's supposed to be quite interesting.'

★ ★ ★

The leaflet was right; Beddgelert is a 'pretty' village. Just past the *Welcome To* sign I do a sharp left and take us over a small, hump-backed bridge. I park next to a primary school, get the wheelchair out and help Pete into it.

'Gelert's grave,' I say. 'That's where the name comes from. The bed of Gelert.' I point towards a field behind a gallery selling arts and crafts. 'It should be just over there.'

I push Pete across a narrow cattle grid and out towards the start of a concrete path that runs alongside a river. Halfway along the path, where the dry-stone wall ends, I veer off to the right into the muddy field. My feet skid on the mud. Only the handles of the chair keep me upright.

In the centre of the field, a group of people dressed in blue jackets are gathered around two trees. As we approach them I realise they're a family. The father, standing facing the eldest boy, keeps placing the palms of his hands on the boy's cheeks. The boy doesn't like the game and he repeatedly pushes the hands away. In the end, frustrated, he steps back and almost slips on the mud. 'Stop it, Dad,' he says. The father laughs but the boy doesn't.

We join them and they form a respectful clearing for the wheelchair. They hang around for a while, then walk away.

The grave, in-between the two trees, is a large boulder that an image of a curled up dog has been carved into. There are two new-looking granite plaques, one at the base of each tree, the left one in English, the right in Welsh. A metal fence circles everything.

'Can you read the inscription from there?' I ask.

'I'm cold.'

'We'll find a café.'

'I saw a pub near the bridge.'

The story is shamelessly sentimental but I read it out loud anyway: 'In the 13th Century, Llewellyn Prince of North Wales was out hunting. When the Prince returned, his dog, Gelert, came to meet him, his muzzle covered in blood. Alarmed, the Prince went to search for his infant son, and when he saw that the cot was empty and surrounded by blood-soaked blankets, he killed the dog with his sword. The dog's dying yelp was answered by the cry of the infant, which the Prince found in an adjoining room, lying next to a dead wolf that Gelert had fought off and killed. Unable to forgive himself, the Prince never smiled again. And he buried the dog here.'

'So he messed up. Am I supposed to feel sorry for him?'

'I do,' I say, 'a bit.'

Pete pats his pockets, an unlit cigarette dangling from his mouth. 'Was my lighter in the car? I can't find it.'

'No idea.'

'I must have lost it.'

We hang around the grave until Pete says he's ready to leave. I push him back across the field, taking a path I didn't spot earlier. It leads us back to the same cattle-grid. I stop to let a couple across. Their black greyhound is hesitating. The woman urges it on. 'Come on, Wilson. Come on, lad.' She crouches and slaps her thigh. Wilson shivers, the thin skin on his ribs twitching, his sad eyes darting from one face to another — the woman's, the man's, mine, Pete's. He steps tentatively onto the grid and makes it halfway across, but then his back legs slip between the girders and he goes down. I look at Pete. His face is a picture of heartbreak. He is the dog. His whole life has been one long cattle-grid.

Our tour of the village is a short one. We look in shop windows and linger in doorways. I buy a flapjack. Pete buys some matches and a postcard of a mountain range at sunset to send to Iris. 'Do you think she'll get it before — ' he breaks off. 'When are we planning to go back to London?'

'Tomorrow. That okay?'

'He nods thoughtfully. 'I'll send it today.'

★　★　★

We see three more sites, and the third is the closest match of the day. The road is perfect, the lake the right size, and it ends before the bend. A mountain rises up on our left, and where Pete remembers the slip road to be is a gate, which I climb over.

'It's just grass. A field,' I shout.

Smoke darts from his mouth, sucked by the wind through the wound down window. 'Maybe there used to be a path,' he shouts back.

I shake my head. 'I doubt it.' I examine the ground more closely, looking for ridges. 'No. I'm fairly certain there was never a path here.'

★　★　★

We are back in the bunkhouse and I've made peanut butter sandwiches with white, thick-sliced bread. Pete has nibbled at one but is too tired to eat any more.

I help him onto the bed, and while he sleeps I pin up the map and fix the Polaroids to their matched locations. Five sites. Another five tomorrow.

I wake him at 7.30 and suggest we go for a drink. He says he needs to take a shower, so I carry him down the stairs. I set the water temperature. Then I place a red plastic chair directly under the line of fire and he obediently sits on it.

'The chair matches your cast,' I point out. 'You're colour-coordinated.'

★   ★   ★

Out of the three pubs we looked at, the one we've chosen is called The Waterfront. Two girls at the bar giggle when I roll Pete up next to them. He notices but couldn't care less.

Again, there are pictures of walkers every-where. And next to the bar is a sign reading CLIMBING WALL, a chalk arrow pointing to a blue door. I wheel Pete around to take a look. Inside a low-ceilinged room the length of a bus, half a dozen men and women hang from the sloping walls, their hands white with chalk, the veins in their forearms bulging. We watch for a while until Pete sighs heavily and turns away. 'Why would anyone want to do that in a pub?'

I order baked salmon and a pint of Guinness. Pete opts for haddock and chips and a pint of Carlsberg. During the next twenty-five minutes he drinks two more pints and eats nothing of the food.

'Come on,' I say. 'The fish looks pretty good. Try some of it. Just a little.'

'I can't be bothered.'

I set down my glass. 'Do you know anything about eating disorders? Sarah has one. It used to be pretty bad, apparently.'

'How do you think she's doing?'

'Okay, I hope.'

'It was nice of her to lend us the car.'

I nod and drink off some of the Guinness. 'How about you? Do you think *you* might have an eating disorder?'

He laughs and sprays beer over the table. 'Don't be ridiculous. I've never hated myself like that. People who stuff their faces hate themselves, and it's probably the same with the ones who choose to starve. I don't eat because there's no point. I'd only be fighting a losing battle. I dread to think what my insides look like. Grey, I imagine. Battered haddock is no match for what's going on in there, no matter how good it looks.'

Before we leave, twenty minutes (and three more pints for Pete) later, he asks at the bar if it's possible to buy a bottle of wine. The barman asks what type. Pete points down at his cast. The barman peers over the bar and smiles. 'House red.'

* * *

When we pull up outside the bunkhouse it's still only 9.30 but feels like the middle of the night. I carry Pete up to the room and sit him down on the top bunk next to the window. 'Don't smoke,' I say. 'I'm going to ask Maggie if she'd like to come up and have a drink with us.'

Maggie says she'd love to join us, and as though keen to demonstrate how much, she whistles cheerfully as we crunch across the gravel. 'It's nice to get to know the people who stay,' she says as we climb the stairs. 'I usually wait to be asked. I don't like to force myself on people. You never know with couples, do you?'

'No,' I say. 'I suppose not.'

Maggie and I sit on the floor in the centre of the room. She pours the wine into the three heavy green tumblers she brought up with her. I give one to Pete, who's still up on the bunk staring out of the window.

'I never used to drink until I met Jesse,' Maggie chuckles. 'But I do now.'

I raise my glass. 'Cheers.'

She raises hers. 'To fresh air.'

I ask Pete if he'd like to come down from the bunk. He nods.

Maggie smiles kindly at him. 'There's not much to see out there at night,' she says. 'Just dark fields, I'm afraid.'

I lift him down, and as I'm setting him into a wicker armchair, Maggie's face softens. She looks like she's about to say something. But then she decides not to.

We talk for a while about how beautiful the pass down into the village is. Then, when there's a lull, Maggie cranes her neck to look at the map and Polaroids.

'What is that?' she asks. 'Is it something to do with your work?'

'No,' I say. 'Not really. I'm an artist.'

'Oh,' she says. 'Do you make a living at it?'

'Yes, but you know, I'm not a millionaire.'

She shakes her head. 'It must be hard. I think it's a shame for all the ones that don't.'

'It is a bit of a struggle at times,' I say. 'Not the wisest career choice. I suppose I've been pretty lucky.'

She smiles. 'And what are your paintings like?'

'Some are funny, some are sad, some are both.'

'So not abstract.'

'Oh, you know a bit about art, then?'

Maggie looks at the map again. 'My first husband was an artist. He used to do these lovely drawings of buildings in black ink. But he'd sometimes use brown ink on the lines, to soften them, you know, make them look old.'

'Sepia,' Pete says.

'That's right. Exactly. That's how they looked. He died ten years ago. We lived in Essex then. And do you know what? When he died, everyone wanted to buy one. Typical. I suppose that makes him a *real* artist, doesn't it. I sold most of them. I wish I hadn't now. I'd show you the ones I have left but I'm not sure where they are.'

Pete wriggles in his chair. He moves his cast leg to the side by lifting it with both hands. 'How long have you and Jesse been married?'

'Six years.'

'I've been married twice too.'

Maggie looks confused, then says, 'Jesse's actually my third husband.'

I pick up the half full bottle of wine. Pete holds out his tumbler and I half fill it. Maggie does the same. 'My second husband was a photographer,' she goes on. 'He *photographed* buildings. What about that? My first husband did some paintings based on some of the photographs taken by my second husband. They knew each other, you see. They were already friends. Everyone thinks that's strange. It is a bit of a long story. My first husband took a long time to die, you see. He had cancer and his friend and I used to take turns in looking after him. That's how we got together. My husband knew we were seeing each other, but he said he didn't mind. He knew he was dying. He was an amazing man. Not a selfish bone in his body.'

'My mum died of cancer just before Christmas,' I say. 'I don't think Christmas will ever be the same again. We had three different types of greetings card up. *Merry Christmas. Get Well Soon. Sorry For Your Loss.* It was all pretty weird. My girlfriend's sister died of it too. A couple of weeks ago. She was only thirty-one.'

Maggie looks at me, her brow wrinkled. 'Your girlfriend?'

'Yes.'

'Oh.' She looks at Pete and bites her bottom lip. 'So you two, you're not . . . ' she smiles nervously.

Pete grins. 'Not what? A couple?'

Maggie nods.

'No,' he says. 'We're bloody not.'

'Sorry. I thought, you know, you being ill . . .'

Pete laughs out loud. 'You thought I had AIDS.'

'I'm sorry.' She grimaces, a display of embarrassment. The veins in her neck look like the roots of a small tree. She drops her shoulders and shakes her head at herself.

Pete drains his glass and sets it down next to him. 'We're actually brothers,' he says.

Maggie looks confused. 'But you have different surnames. I saw it in the register. Do you mean half brothers? Sorry, I hope you don't think I'm prying.'

'No,' Pete says. 'Not half brothers. Full brothers.' He looks at me. 'Tell her if you like. I don't mind.'

I do. In the next ten or so minutes I tell her everything, the whole story, and the words come easily because she's a total stranger. Once I'm done the room grows quiet for a while, so I excuse myself to use the toilet. Preferring the open air to the cramped, chemical smelling cubicle downstairs, I venture outside.

It's very quiet, the only sound is of distant cars. I piss against the wall. Then I walk blindly back towards the bunkhouse. Halfway there I stumble over something, and when I stretch out both arms, my hands meet two smooth long objects, which I soon realise are the catamarans I saw earlier (Jesse obviously moved them). I stay bent over them for a while, suddenly aware of the wine and the sleepy fog it has brought in. I sit down, and the fibreglass hulls creak under my weight.

Sarah's Mini is glowing eerily in the light from Maggie's kitchen. Beyond the car park I can see the village in the distance, a row of twinkling orange lights. The sky is black and purple, the horizon a wide band of pink.

I stand and head back upstairs.

While I've been away Pete has laid down on the floor and his head is resting on Maggie's lap. His eyes are closed and he's smiling. Maggie is stroking his hair. 'You just never know what's happened in people's lives,' she says. 'We were just saying. I think the two of you should write a book together. I'd definitely read it.'

I sit down, cross-legged. 'How did you and Jesse meet, Maggie?'

Pete's eyes open. My mention of Jesse has slashed a hole in the fabric of a perfect moment.

'Believe it or not he was another distant friend of my first two husbands. I've known of him all my life, really. He was with someone else for twenty years, the woman he should have spent the rest of his life with. She let him down, though. And Jesse's not the type of man who likes being let down. He was up in Scotland cycling and was hit by a car and left for dead. He ended up in hospital in Fort William, in a coma, well, a kind of coma, for almost two weeks. When he came round he was sent home, but he was bedbound for a long time afterwards. He couldn't do much for himself, and his wife couldn't cope. Some people just can't, can they? Some people aren't good with illness or disability. They don't know how to be. She left him in the end. I'd already been through it all before, so *I* didn't mind visiting him. Looking at him now, you'd never believe he almost died. Would you?'

'No,' I say. 'How old is he?'

'Seventy-two.'

'He's amazing for his age.'

Maggie laughs. 'He's a bit eccentric. Maybe he's got dementia. His favourite quirk is to pretend his ideas really *are* his. Most of them are mine. He does that all the time, and I let him. Did you expect him to be wearing a cowboy hat?' She removes her glasses and wipes them. 'He does in spirit. He still goes up to the top of Snowdon every now and again, but he admits he doesn't find it as easy as he used to. We have an eighteen inch metal plate above the fireplace. They removed it from his leg after two years. He has long legs. Sexy legs, I think. Still.'

* * *

Maggie has left us and we are in our beds watching a documentary about the history of Blackpool Pleasure Beach. Some old black and white footage of the construction of the rollercoaster is playing. A man hammers a huge wedge in-between two railway sleepers. He straightens up, takes off his cap, wipes his brow, and grins at the camera.

I drain off the last of my wine and put the glass on the bedside table. 'What would you say was the cruelest thing you've ever done?'

Pete thinks for a moment. 'I can't think of anything. Apart from the things I did to myself, which you already know about. Why, what about you?'

'When I was about eight, me and a friend lied to an autistic boy that the fair had come to town. His name was Andrew Gray. He lived on my street. My dad had brought some planks of wood home and we took them to a piece of old wasteland. We propped one up on a fence — a slide — and tied others together with bits of rope to make a climbing frame. We didn't mean anything by lying to him. We just thought he'd appreciate our efforts. He obviously did because that evening he came back with his dad. His dad had dressed up for the occasion. He was wearing a grey suit. I'm sure he knew all along that there was nothing special going on but he went along with it anyway, just to make his son happy.'

Pete nods. 'That's the kind of thing my dad would have done.'

'He sounds like a good man.'

'He was. He was the best dad anyone could wish for. He made a kite for me when I was six. We were flying it and I let go of the lines. He didn't tell me off. We just chased it for a long time. It didn't go too high for a while and we thought we might get it. But then the wind took it and we had to give up. He was as upset as I was and said we could make another, but for some reason we never got round to it.'

'I have a kite. I actually have it with me. In the car.'

'Why?'

'What do you mean, why?'

'You're a grown man.'

'It's relaxing. You should try it.'

'What's *he* like, then — our father who isn't in heaven?'

'He has a bit of a temper. Never admits he's wrong. But, you know, he's my dad. *Our* dad.'

Pete shakes his head. 'I'll never think of him that way. He doesn't deserve it. Are you going to tell him about me?'

'Of course. I don't know how though.'

'What do you think he'll say?'

'I've no idea. He's pretty unpredictable.'

'And what about *her*? What was she like?'

'Mum? She was a good cook and loved the countryside. She was happiest picking blackberries and making pies. She did have a dark side though. She liked to read about serial killers. Her favourite film was *Silence of the Lambs*.'

'Does *he* read?'

'No. I don't think I ever saw him read a book.'

'Did you ever see him cry?'

'Yes. But he didn't know I was there. He was in the garage. His dad had died the week before.'

'If he were here now, crying and wanting to spill his guts, do you know what I'd say to him? I'd tell him to go and fuck himself.'

I nod. 'That's understandable. I felt the same way when I found out about you. But it's kind of passed now and turned into sadness.'

'They didn't dump you though, did they?'

'No.' I pull the covers up to my chin. 'When Sarah told you how they'd met — the car crash — what did you think? As coincidences go, that's pretty up there.'

'There's no such thing as coincidences. More like transferred karma. They met through a car crash, some of the bad energy went into creating me, and the remainder killed my adopted mother eight years later because she stepped in and tried to put things right.'

'You don't seriously believe that.'

'One hundred per cent. I'm cursed. I always was. You can't kill energy; it just goes somewhere else. Nothing that starts badly ever ends well.'

Maybe it's the alcohol, but I can't help thinking his theory makes sense. 'And what about me? Where do I fit in?'

'You'll have to work that out for yourself. You've changed since we met. That's a start.'

'Really? How?'

'You're a bit less sarcastic, easier to talk to. I wasn't sure about you at first but I'm glad you're my brother.'

'You're drunk.'

'Maggie's nice. She doesn't seem old.'

'No.'

'You can never have too many friends.'

I nod. 'True.'

'I wouldn't say it if it wasn't. I wish I'd had more.'

19

Take the Rough with the Smooth,
(oil, or possibly acrylic, on canvas)

A butcher with my dad's features stands staring wistfully out of a window. There are tears in his eyes and his face is ashen. Next to him is a chopping table, half of which has been sanded clean, its history erased. Turned on its side on the other half — still scarred and chipped from knives and cleavers — is a battered Quality Street tin with bric-a-brac and old photographs spilling out of it.

We've decided not to start the day checking out remaining crash sites. First we'll find another hotel, something more comfortable where Pete can smoke undetected.

He sits up in bed. 'I don't feel too good. Could you get me some toilet roll?'

I bring him a wad and he coughs up what look like blood clots.

'How long has that been happening?'

'It happens all the time. Ulcer.'

'You have an ulcer?'

'I wouldn't be surprised. I've got everything else.'

'We should get you to a doctor.'

'What for? To tell me what I already know? I'm sick of doctors. I came here to get away from all that.'

I draw back the curtain and look at the weather. It's dry but cloudy — and judging by the sway of the trees, pretty windy. 'Let's go over onto Anglesey later,' I say. 'We can fly the kite.'

Pete finds the remote in the folds of his blankets. He points and presses but nothing happens.

'It's off at the socket,' I say.

* * *

I bundle our things together, and after Pete's eaten a fried egg, I carry him down to the car. When I go to the house to pay for our stay Maggie insists on coming out with me to say goodbye. Pete doesn't hide how pleased he is to see her and he winds down the window.

Maggie smiles. 'I hope we'll see you again.' She leans in through the window and pecks him on the cheek. 'Good luck with everything.'

He beams. 'Thanks.'

'We're taking the day off,' I say. 'Going to

269

the beach with a kite.'

'Lovely.'

'You're a nice woman,' Pete says.

Maggie's smile is motherly. 'And you're a nice man.'

★ ★ ★

I head back towards Llanberis. We drive back over the pass and turn right at Capel Curig. Pete rolls a cigarette and pats his shirt pocket. 'Now I've lost my *other* lighter. I had it earlier.'

'What colour is it?'

'Purple. Transparent.'

'Try the floor.'

'No, I had it up in the room.'

'There might be some matches in the foot-well. Sarah uses them when she goes camping.'

He leans forward and begins rummaging among the papers, muesli bar wrappers, water bottles, cassettes, books and computer cables. We round a bend and I see a sign — HOTEL PEN-Y-GWRYD 100m and I turn right down a narrow track. Trees claw at my window. We round a blind bend and the hotel comes into view.

'This place looks okay,' I say.

I pull into the car park and stop.

The hotel is a small grey slate cottage

circled by black railings and daffodils. A steep grassy hill rises up immediately behind it. The front door is framed by a clumsy looking mosaic made from shells. The gate hangs open, the top hinge broken. Smoke rises from the chimney.

'Any luck?'

Shaking his head, Pete comes back up to sitting. But when he sees the hotel he freezes, his eyes wide, the cigarette hanging limply from his bottom lip.

'What's wrong?' I ask.

'This is the hotel we stayed in.'

★ ★ ★

For the next few minutes he smokes in silence and gradually some of the colour returns to his cheeks. Even then, though, he's still not sure he can stay here. It may be too much, might taint the few good memories he has.

'We can just take a look,' I suggest. 'If you don't like how it feels, we can leave.'

'It hasn't changed at all. Even that crawler around the window looks the same.'

'If this is the hotel, maybe the site is nearby. Can you remember how long you'd been driving when you crashed?'

'No.'

'Let me know when you're ready. Take your time.'

★ ★ ★

The girl at reception agrees to show us the upstairs room, 'the one where you can actually touch the mountain by leaning out of the window'. She smiles at Pete's description and tells us that everyone loves that room.

'Let me just double-check for you,' she says in her soft Welsh accent. 'I think it's free, but I'd best make sure.' She flips through the book. 'Yes. It's available.'

Pete looks up at me from the wheelchair. He looks frightened suddenly, very small down there.

I lift him up and jiggle him in my arms until I find a comfortable carrying position. Then I follow the girl up the stairs. They are wider than at Jesse's. Easy. Nothing to bang his leg on. His face so close to mine, it's impossible to escape the smell of his breath. Alcohol and cigarettes, and somehow, onion. His forearm, in contrast to my pink fingers encircling it, looks yellow, jaundiced.

After two flights we come to a small landing. The girl stops. 'Mind the steps here,' she says. 'There's no carpet and it can be a bit slippy.' Light floods in through a small arched window at the end of the landing. A diagonal shaft of dust particles lights up a square of wall. We move into the shaft and it warms my back. On the windowsill are a pitcher and bowl and two pottery cats.

We climb another flight of stairs and come out onto a grey-carpeted landing with pink-papered walls. The girl pauses outside one of the doors and turns to me. 'So, when was it that you stayed here?'

'Not me.'

'You, sir?'

Pete nods. 'A long time ago.'

She glances at his leg, the bit of cast near his ankle where Maggie signed her name — *All the best for the future, Maggie.* She turns the key and pushes the door open. I carry Pete over to one of the single beds and lower him down. 'Has it changed much?'

'There was only one bed then,' he says. 'A double. We all slept in it.'

The girl opens the curtains. 'We always have two singles now. That way, couples can have them apart, or if they want to, they can push them together.'

'That's new.' Pete points to a small en-suite bathroom.

The girl folds her arms. 'Yes, my dad built it. About fifteen years ago now.'

Pete slides himself over to the window.

'That's what I remember most clearly. The side of the mountain.' Outside, only an arms length away from the glass, grass and rich green ferns are the only view. 'Can we open it?' he asks.

'Of course.' The girl walks over to the window, stoops, flips up the catch and pushes it open.

Pete shakes his head. 'Exactly the same.'

'Yes,' the girl says. 'That never seems to change much.' She looks at me and smiles cheerfully.

'Me and Norma used to climb out and just lie there.' He turns to me. 'This room's on the cactus drawing. It's one of the pink ones, about a third of the way up.'

The girl nods politely, despite not understanding.

'Did you get the floor plan right?' I ask him.

He looks around and then nods towards a small round table with a box of tissues on it. 'I don't think I got that alcove. Apart from that, yes.'

'Shall I leave you to think about it?' the girl asks.

'No,' Pete says. 'We'll take it.'

'Great. Come back to reception when you've got your things up.'

'How old are you?' Pete suddenly asks her out of the blue.

'I'm twenty-nine, sir,' she says, smiling.

'You look much younger. Is your mother here? I mean, does she live here?'

'Yes she does. She's upstairs.'

'Do you think she'd come down for a minute? I'd like to ask her something. About local history. Do you think she'd mind?'

'I can go and ask her. I'm sure she will help if she can.'

It turns out that she can, and less than five minutes later we are sitting with her in the cosy living room downstairs, a fire roaring in the dog grate. She has the same warmth as Maggie and looks like the type of woman who takes long coastline walks, paints watercolours, or makes clay coil-pots. The daughter goes off to make tea while Pete explains about the nature of our trip. The woman shakes her head sadly. Then she tells us what she remembers.

The crash made the local newspapers, and although it was a quarter of a century ago, it's still fairly fresh in her mind. It happened around lunchtime on a Thursday. She knows it was a Thursday because she used to drive into Llanberis to pick up the weekly supply of fruit and veg. The road was closed off that particular Thursday, and police were waving back the traffic. There was no alternative route, so she had to wait until late afternoon to make her trip.

The van driver was a local man in his 40s. He was still drunk from the night before. He died at the scene, along with Pete's mother. The man's wife had recently left him to move in with her much younger lover. She'd taken their three children with her.

As the woman tells the story I'm surprised by my reaction. I feel only a little sadness for Pete's mother, and much more for the van driver. He's the one that strikes a chord with me. Somehow he seems like the only three dimensional character. Despite all the chaos he left behind — chaos that twenty-five years later has led, in a roundabout way, to my employment as my brother's carer — I see him as the antithesis of our own dad. He had his children taken away from him; he didn't give them up.

The woman describes how to get to the crash site, Cowis bend, a notorious accident black spot. 'You must have taken it on the way to the hotel,' she tells us. 'Still, after all these years, it's the only road you can take.'

* * *

I take our bags up to the room. Then we leave. As we drive away, I can't help but worry. Now that we know where to find the site, should we really go there? Shouldn't we

276

simply turn around and head back to London? Wouldn't that be for the best?

'No,' Pete says. 'We came this far so we may as well finish it. I was just in the room where she spent her last night. I may as well see where she died.'

The road forks up ahead and I bear right, skirting around Llanberis rather than passing through it. We sweep around the lake for five or so minutes, and then up ahead I spot the landmark the woman described — a T-shaped rock jutting out of the high grass bank. I slow down and roll up the bend. There's a lay-by and I pull into it.

Neither of us get out or say a word. We just sit there and take in the details. Oddly enough, the place bears only a little resemblance to either the drawings or the model. There doesn't appear to be a slip road at all, and the only water I can see is the huge expanse of the lake. I look up at the bank. Yes, there are trees up there, trees that would have been smaller but present nonetheless when our tragic van driver rounded the bend and caught sight of the car that would kill him. Apart from that, though, we could be anywhere.

Anywhere.

Somewhere.

Nowhere.

A map of nowhere. That's what Pete

sketched. He sketched a place and had no idea where it was, couldn't for the life of him remember. It could have been anywhere in the country, anywhere from Land's End to John O'Groats.

But it's here.

We are Now Here.

NowHere.

I look at Pete. There are tears in his eyes but they have yet to break free. I look at the road, then up at the trees again. For this we came more than two hundred miles.

I once went to the Grand Canyon and remember feeling this way. Looking across to the other rim, ten miles in the distance, I thought to myself: 'okay, how long should I stand here in order to fully appreciate what I'm seeing?'

I look at Pete again. Tears are now streaming down his cheeks. I take a packet of tissues from the glove compartment and pass one to him.

'Do you need to stay for a little while?'

He shakes his head. 'No, that's enough now.'

★ ★ ★

Ten minutes later, still not a word said between us, I'm taking the car back up towards Jesse and Maggie's bunkhouse. As we pass by, Pete cranes his neck in an attempt to hang onto it for as long as possible.

I head out towards Bangor. We wind down through a pine forest. Pete rests his head against the window and sighs.

'You okay?'

'Mmm.'

'You sure?'

'Mmm.'

But he clearly isn't.

We drive in silence for a while. I take one of Sarah's CDs from the inside of the door and push it into the slot. There's a pause, and then loud, distorted Hindi music fills the car. Pete doesn't flinch. I turn the volume down and hear a helicopter. I bend forwards and spot it to our left. It's yellow. 'Mountain rescue,' I say.

Nothing.

The forest thins, then ends, and we turn right onto a busy road. The traffic, noise and pylons seem to signal the end of something.

We drop downhill, towards the Menai Bridge. On the far bank are hundreds of square houses — most white, some blue, one yellow. On the straits, fishing boats move between bright orange buoys.

Once we're across the bridge I pull into a petrol station to look at the map. The white

VW Camper from yesterday is on the fore-court. Pete glances at it and shakes his head.

'I'll head for Newborough,' I say. 'It's on the southern tip of the island.'

'How much further?'

'Ten minutes maybe.'

⋆　⋆　⋆

We drive for two or three miles and then turn right down a narrow road. Up ahead, a strait of sand and water come into view. A high wall on our right reflects the sound of the engine back at us, doubling it. Sarah's exhaust may need looking at.

After half a mile or so the road ends and we find ourselves on a muddy track that will lead us into a farmyard if we continue. I pull over next to a gate with a Private Property sign on it. High up on the grass bank above are what look like holiday homes, behind them rows and rows of static caravans.

The sun comes out. I open the door and take off my shoes and socks. The only sound is the gentle splashing of a small nearby boat that bobs between two high walls.

'This isn't the place we're heading for,' I say. 'But it's fine for a tea break.'

Pete opens his door. 'There's not much wind for your kite. Look.' He points at the boat's pink flag. It flutters to life, then dies.

'I'll take another look at the map in a minute,' I say, handing him the flask. 'It should be windier up on the north coast. It's the Irish Sea.'

I get him into the wheelchair and push him to the edge of the road which overlooks a sheer drop down to some seaweed filled pools. I leave him there and head back towards the car. 'Make sure you've got the brake on,' I call over my shoulder. 'I'm not going in there after you.'

Sitting in the drivers seat I unfold the map on the steering wheel. As far as I can make out, we are across from Caernarfon inside a two inch red box: WARNING! PUBLIC RIGHT OF WAY CAN BE DANGEROUS UNDER TIDAL CONDITIONS.

I fold the map, rejoin Pete and we sit for a while looking out across the strait — a narrow strip of water, everything beyond it sand. A car crawls up the road behind us and parks in front of the holiday homes. Two old couples get out and slowly make their way up the concrete steps.

Pete exhales smoke out over the water. 'I never want to talk about your parents again,' he says. 'That's what they are, as far as I'm concerned — *your* parents. My parents are the two people I came here with twenty-five years ago. But they're both dead now.'

'Okay,' I say. 'I understand.'

He turns towards me. 'Do you want to die quickly?'

'I don't want to die at all.'

'But you will. And when you do, do you want it to be quick?'

'Doesn't everyone?'

'I don't know about everyone. I just know about me. I'm not frightened of being dead. But I am nervous about the dying part, the trip from here to there. It's best to make it a quick journey, don't you think, so that you don't have time to change your mind? A long, frightened trip wouldn't be something I'd want.'

'You mean if you take your own life?'

'No, not necessarily. Don't worry, I don't feel like doing that anymore.'

'Good.'

'I don't know how I'll die,' he says. 'But I know it won't be in a rest-home with old people. I know that much. Iris' mum died on a plane coming back from Ireland. Heart attack. One minute she's looking at the clouds, the next minute she's in them. I wonder how many people die on planes. I mean apart from in crashes. When *I* die, you'll be able to get on with your life again. You'll be stronger. Like when siamese twins are separated and the healthy one gets back what the weaker one was draining away.'

'Don't be stupid,' I say. 'I don't even think that's the right way round. And anyway, how can you have been draining anything from me? I've only known you for five months.'

'Badness is stronger than time. Time doesn't mean anything. My badness has probably been messing things up for you all your life without you even knowing it.'

'I wouldn't say that my life *has* been messed up.'

'No? Tell me this, then. Throughout your life has it felt like someone has been opening doors for you or closing them in your face? Go on, be honest.'

'Opening them, mostly. I've been lucky.'

'Great. Good for you. Open Door. How perfect. When I'm gone things might get even better. You should make something out of our story. Don't waste it. People love a tragedy — as long as it's not their own.'

★ ★ ★

Fifteen minutes later we've cut diagonally across the island and entered Benllech. Driving barefoot has helped lift my spirits, create a holiday feel. Above the rooflines of more box houses the sea finally comes into view on our right. We turn at a café with a giant fibreglass effigy of a chef outside it and begin our descent, through an estate, to the seafront road.

I park in the mostly empty car park behind a silver 4×4 that has its heavy looking back door open. A woman is on all fours inside the roomy boot folding blankets and children's clothes. She climbs out, turns a pair of small Wellington boots upside down, and bangs them together. Streams of sand drift in the wind.

Sitting side on in the driver's seat I roll up my jeans. I get Pete into the wheelchair and give him the bagged kite. He places it on his lap.

The seafront is classic British, though on a small scale. A few bright lights and some washed out, pastel coloured paint. In the BAHAMA GIFT SHOP I buy a fridge magnet for myself (a miniature plate of spaghetti bolognese with a fork stuck in it) and another kite for Pete — cheaper quality than mine but okay.

I push him down the concrete ramp and out onto the sand. The wheelchair struggles in the deeper parts. The beach is fairly quiet, the wind strong. High on the grass bank to our left are more static caravans.

A white plastic bag comes tumbling across the sand towards us. All this open space and it finds Pete's foot.

'Fuck off,' he says, kicking it free.

We slowly head towards the waters edge where the waves are crashing in, determined, unstoppable, the way they will continue to crash in when both of us are long gone. I picture the model bobbing away on one. A farewell to something beautiful but ruinous.

We pass a huge L that someone has scraped into the sand. Then an O. Then a V. Then an E. Just beyond the E, I stop and put the wheelchair's brake on. I sit down on the sand. Pete tries to light a cigarette but the wind is too strong. I kneel next to him and cup my hands around the match. Before long he's puffing away.

'I'll be back in a minute,' I tell him, and I get to my feet.

He nods.

I walk into the water and paddle around for a while, watching foam circle my ankles and thinking about Clare's ashes in the sea on the other side of the world. I miss her more than I miss Sarah. At least you always knew where you were with her.

After a while I look over my shoulder. Pete's no longer smoking. He's just sitting there, bored, wanting time to pass.

I walk back over to him and begin unpacking the new kite. 'The only thing you can get wrong is the tying on of the strings,' I say. 'About five times on each side is fine.'

'How difficult to fly are they?'

'Not at all. They look it but aren't.'

'Are they the ones you can do tricks with?'

'Stunts.' I tie a knot and pull to tighten it.

Once the kite is fully assembled I explain the basic principles. Pull on the right line to make a downward dive to the right. Pull left for left. Simple. To make the kite hover directly above you, hold the hoops apart, arms out to the side — like Jesus on the cross.

I pass the hoops to him and start to back away. 'When I throw it up, pull the handgrips towards your chest. And hold on tight.'

Right on cue, the wind comes sweeping in off the water. I throw the kite up and it soars.

'That's right,' I shout. 'Don't try anything fancy. Just keep it up there.' I sprint towards him. 'Hang on, I'll show you what to do.'

I let the kite hover for a while. Then I make several dives, one of which I come out of by sweeping the kite horizontally at head height. The nylon flaps and rattles, machine-like. I lie down on my back, my arms apart, the kite hanging directly above us. The sand feels cold. I should have brought a jumper.

I get to my feet and pass the handgrips back to him. 'Try some steering.'

'No, I'm okay with it like this.'

'Come on. Anyone can make it hover. Hovering's easy.'

'I like easy.'

But he does try some steering eventually, and he's good at it, much better than I was at first. He has a feel for it, seems to know instinctively how hard or gently to pull. Good right/left awareness. Sound coordination. The kite does come down a few times, but each time it does he calls for my help.

After a while I notice that the plastic rods have torn through the fabric and are protruding at the kite's tip.

I throw it up again. 'You can tell it's only a cheap one,' I shout. 'It's damaged already. When you crash it down, try to do it gently.'

'How am I supposed to crash it down gently?'

'I'm joking.'

'Oh.'

I leave him and unpack my kite, which I then assemble. I lay it down on the sand and back away from it, willing the wind not to flip it over before I manage to get the lines taut. After a few failed attempts I get it up, and it takes me a while to get a feel for it. It has so much more pull than the cheaper one, feels heavier and more responsive. I call out to Pete to ask if he's okay. He says he is, so I back away from him, keeping a close eye on the two sets of lines to make sure they don't get too close and tangle.

I turn and head along the beach towards an outcrop of black rock. I pass a man carrying a bucket; behind him his small daughter is walking backwards, dragging a plastic spade, making swirls in the sand. I look over my shoulder to check Pete's kite is still up.

I paddle through some shallow pools and head around the outcrop into a small, secluded bay surrounded by black, oily looking cliffs. The wind isn't as strong here. I'm shielded. Protected. I change direction and walk towards the sea. Above the outcrop, around the bay, I can see Pete's kite swaying gently from side to side. Nothing too risky. No daring moves.

Lost in the swooping of my own kite, life feels good, uncomplicated, stripped back to its bare bones. Tomorrow, when we head home, it may well be to a whole new life, a blank canvas. A new place to live. A brother to introduce to friends. A different woman in my life? But no job (Phil may be open-minded and flexible, but only up to a point).

I try a few loops with the kite and manage three or four before it gets too low and almost touches down. I take it up again and keep it there, gently swaying from side to side. I notice that Pete's kite does the same. I hold my handgrips apart and make it hang. His hangs.

We are brothers. This is intimacy.

After a while I decide to start back. He's probably keen for a drink, and I need to eat something. As I near the outcrop more of the beach comes into view, and more of Pete's lines. Any second now he will appear, my strange little older brother, and when he does, and when I call out to him, I'm hoping for a conspiratorial wink or an ear-to-ear grin. I want him to be happy. God knows he deserves to be. I want this day to be one he remembers for a long time. The day he and his brother flew kites on a bright May afternoon in Wales.

I splash through the shallow pools, retracing my steps. The top-line of the outcrop lowers, and his lines lengthen. I wade into the sea, knee-deep, and look down at my feet. They look green and dead.

When I look up I spot a teenager in grey combat shorts and a hooded top walking purposefully towards Pete's wheelchair. He suddenly breaks into a jog, and my instinct is to shout out, 'Hey!.. *Hey!* Leave him alone. He can't even walk. He's in a fucking wheelchair! . . . '

But then I notice something isn't right. Pete's slumped forward, his chin against his chest, arms limp by his sides. He doesn't appear to be holding the lines at all — it looks as though he's slipped the hoops up his arms and the pull of the kite has taken them up to his armpits. With each gust of wind, his shoulders lurch and the strong pull lifts him slightly out of the chair like a puppet. I look up at his kite. It drifts gently from side to side. Hangs, drifts, hangs again.

I begin to run, calling out, 'Hey, he's with me, he's with me.' But the teenager is already down on his haunches at Pete's side, lifting his limp head and mouthing something. He pats a cheek gently. Then he slides the hand loops down Pete's arms and casts them to the wind. I look up at the kite. It dies in the air, flutters back to life, then turns and sweeps out towards the sea.

I pray for it to stay airborne, to rise and rise until it's out of sight — because if it does what I think it will, what Pete's soul almost certainly would — splash down lightly, hardly a splash at all — I will have to admit to myself that what I already suspect is real. He's dead. The teenager suspects it too. He looks up at me as I let go of my own kite, which feels symbolic, and only right. The hoops rise magically and the kite veers off towards the cliff face where a group of children point as it sweeps in. It hits, then drops, the line snagging on a protruding rusty length of metal. The light changes suddenly, the sky darkens, but the red buckets swinging from the children's hands seem to fill with light and glow eerily like Chinese lanterns.

I slide to my knees beside the wheelchair and spot an unlit cigarette rolling away across the sand (did he slip the hoops up his arms in order to light it?). His face has softened, there's a half smile on his lips, and the frown lines between his eyebrows are gone. 'He's my brother,' I say to the teenager, who, now he's established Pete isn't breathing, seems to have decided to do nothing at all. 'Call an ambulance,' I tell him. 'Now.'

He shrugs helplessly. 'I don't have my phone. It's on charge back at the hotel.'

I'm about to bark something about him being stupid and possibly the only fucking teenager in the world who doesn't have a phone on him, when I realise I don't have mine on me either. It's in the glove compartment of the car.

'I'll go and get help,' he says, and skids away.

First, I do the right thing, the standard thing, I check for a pulse. Nothing. Then I look inside his mouth for traces of anything he might have taken. I straighten him in the chair and take hold of his wrist again. No, definitely nothing. I put my ear against his mouth, but what with the noise of the waves and the wind, it would be impossible to hear anything, even if he was fighting fit.

His kite bobs in and washes up on the sand. Then it's taken out again. I get to my feet, turn the wheelchair towards the road and push off. A couple and a small boy are watching from the concrete ramp. The boy points and laughs. His mother yanks his arm back down. At the bottom of the ramp I tilt the chair and set the front wheels onto the concrete. A push forward, a slight lift, and I wheel him up onto the pavement. Now on solid ground, I can speed up.

No cars. Clear. I cross the zebra crossing and head towards the car park. A father up ahead pulls his white football-shirted son to the side to let us by. The boy's ice cream topples out of his hand and splats on the pavement.

'Sorry,' I call over my shoulder. 'I can't stop. I have to get to a hospital.'

But once I get us back inside the car I do stop. There's little point rushing anywhere. He's gone. I know the look (I've seen it often enough recently). I sit for a while, listening to the seagulls and the wind, the only other sound my shallow and rapid breathing. I pick up his hand. Already it's cool and waxy, like

Clare's was. I put it back in his lap, cross it over the other hand, and as I'm about to cover his legs with the blanket I notice the corner of a piece of paper sticking out of his pocket.

I look at it, hoping it isn't a suicide note; I'm not sure I have the guts for that, not sure I want to know his final thoughts. I slip it out anyway. Even before I fully unfold it, I can already see what it is — the DP/PD design I sketched for us on the boat.

Feeling hollowed out and on the verge of tears, I start the engine and pull out of the car park. I head back up the hill, passing rows of bungalows, palm trees in front gardens, gnomes, ponds, elaborate orange sheds with neat asphalt roofs. If the mountain rescue helicopter were overhead now, the pilot would look down and see a tiny white Mini overtaking a parked car, then narrowly missing a cyclist. I look up at the sky. Directly above us two plane vapour trails have made an almost perfect X on the bright blue, as though to mark our exact location, pinpoint The End.

I turn left at the T-junction and drive for a while without knowing where I'm going. But then, before committing myself to the dual carriageway up ahead, I decide it's probably best to stop and check the map.

I pull over and try to calm myself.

Focussing on the map seems to help. I sit for a while, watching traffic go by. I look at Pete and a wave of almost unbearable loneliness hits me. Then unexpected rage.

I take out my phone and scroll to the D's. *Dad* comes up. I take a deep breath, press call, and listen to the ringing with my eyes closed.

'Where are you?' I ask when he finally answers.

'About to get in the car. Hang on (clunk). That's better. I'm at Peterborough races with Eric.'

'I know.'

'Did I tell you? But we only decided to come — '

'I know about the baby you gave away.'

Silence

'Well?'

'How did you find out?'

'I didn't find out. *He* found *me*.'

More silence. Longer this time.

Then, eventually,

'David, let me call you later, once Eric's dropped me off. We can talk about it then. Don't go upsetting — '

'Upsetting?' I say, cutting in on him. 'Let me tell you about upsetting. The brother I only just found out I had is sitting here next to me, dead. That's pretty fucking upsetting.'

With that, I click him to silence. Then I turn my phone off before he has a chance to call back.

I pull out of the lay-by and head back towards Llanberis. I pass a sign for a farm shop that sells 'wheat free bread'. Sarah would love that. Anything that doesn't contain what it should but something weird instead. Milk made from rice or oats. Biscuits sweetened with apple juice. Cornflakes made from rye. Alcohol free wine. Suddenly I remember something, another warning I chose to ignore. Not long after we moved in together the bathroom scales stopped working. Sarah said she'd replaced the batteries but it had made no difference. Like a fool I believed her and we ended up throwing them away.

The weight of a secret, Sarah. What's that?

I sweep around a long curve, my foot now virtually on the floor. Pete's head lolls towards me, and as we come out of the curve it lolls back the other way and cracks against the window. Steering with my right hand, I reach into the back for another blanket which I wedge between his face and the glass. A lorry pulls out of a pub car park and I have to brake sharply. In the distance I can see a range of mountains, black clouds above them, smaller white ones held hostage between the peaks.

Jesse's car park is full, and as we flash by I glance up at the window of our room. The left hand curtain is closed, but I see someone move inside. I'm almost tempted to slam the brakes on, turn around and knock on the door. It would be good to see Maggie and share what's happened. We could have a ceremony. Burn incense. Join hands.

Other, more elaborate ideas come to me in quick succession. Return to the crash site and sit him by the side of the road, a kind of full-circle thing. Or go back to the hotel and sneak him upstairs. Then manhandle him out of the window, return him to the ferns. Bury him in the woods with my bare hands, howling like a wolf by the light of the moon. Take him to the beach at first light, build a raft and push his body out to sea.

I look up at the sky. Afternoon is already beginning to hold suggestions of evening. The air has become smoky and uneven. I need to set off back to London soon, but not in this state.

I pull over and roll to a stop into what will be our last lay-by. I cut the engine, open the door and get out. When I hold my hand out in front, it visibly trembles. I'm cold, my breathing has sped up again, and my scalp feels tight.

I walk a few steps, stop and look down at

my feet. I'm standing only inches away from a sheer drop down into the valley. There's no wall, and a few loose stones fall away and clatter against the rock face. My stomach lurches and I step back. Suicide could never be for me. I'm too much of a coward.

I look to my right where the road snakes up to the top of the pass and eventually disappears between two bright green mounds. Once I've got myself together, I'll make my way up there, then down the other side into Llanberis. The police station shouldn't be hard to find; more difficult will be deciding what to say once I'm standing at the desk. A simple, meat and potatoes account of the facts sounds ridiculous: 'I have a dead man in my car. My brother. He died on the beach over on Anglesey. We were flying kites.'

No, I'll drive him back to London myself. Explanations will have to wait until then. We came here together and that's how we'll leave.

I switch my phone on again and a text comes through telling me I have a new voicemail. I speed dial to listen to it: 'David, it's me. Listen. Please don't blame your mother. Not now. She wanted to tell you, but I stopped her. It was my fault. She never wanted to give up the baby in the first place but I convinced her that it was for the best. We didn't know what we were doing. No-one does when something like that happens. You might — '

I end the call not wanting to hear the rest, and the silence of the valley shocks me. For a few minutes there's nothing, almost less than nothing, but then I hear a car's distant, beelike drone. To my relief, the driver takes another route and the drone changes in pitch and gradually fades away.

I look over at the car. Pete's slumped sideways, his cheek pressed against the window. If I didn't know better, I'd assume he was asleep. Is that what people we'll pass on the motorway will think?

Let them think what they like. Let them assume. As we overtake them in the fast lane let them think we're on the way back from a festival, Pete the worse for wear after pogo-ing himself to the point of exhaustion. Or returning from a heavy stag weekend in Dublin. Something like that. Something fun and normal.

I crunch over to a group of large rocks and sit down on them. High above, a bird of prey hovers. Has it spotted something in the valley and is about to swoop? The only living thing I can see down there is a tiny lone cow by a gate.

For some reason I think about what Maggie said last night, and what Pete said earlier. Maybe I will do something with all of this, once the dust has settled. Write about it. Paint about it. Not for a while though.

I picture myself clearing out his flat. That won't be easy. My brother's clothes, trinkets, cutlery, cups and plates, old hardback books, videos, cheap ornaments, that impressive collection of lighters — the whole lot will have to be boxed up and stored somewhere, and someone else will be moved into Flat A, 54 Warmington Road before he's even cold in the ground.

I lean forward. My lower back feels tight and sore. I get to my feet and stretch. Unexpectedly, I start to cry.

Down in the valley, two sheep have joined the cow by the gate. One limps slightly. The other trots ahead. There we are. The two brothers. Unequal but doing what we can to stick together.

I regret what I said to my dad, and I can see him now, sitting there in the passenger seat as Eric rattles on about horses, blind to my dad's silence, self-hatred, worrying, and desperate brain wracking as to what he can do to put things right.

He's been through enough lately. I'll call him later and let him say his piece. I never was very good at staying angry. It just isn't me.

He and my mother made a bad decision, one which quite possibly ruined their marriage and my mothers health. They paid the price. They were young, had a baby with a deformity, and didn't believe they could cope. They did the opposite of the norm. They refused to accept what they were presented with and take it in their stride. They didn't struggle along, make sacrifices, foot hospital bills, pay for special care, keep smiling, give up ambitions, dreams, careers.

They walked away. They made their decision, stuck with it, and prayed life would be easier that way.

And who am I to judge?

I picture Faye in the park walking towards me stuffing the Bounty into her mouth. No shame. No nibbling in increments. Pure pleasure. Love of the full feeling.

Then I picture sitting down for breakfast every morning with Sarah. Fear in her eyes. Tension in the air. The sound of food being scraped into the bin while I get dressed.

The model is far out at sea now, adrift, a speck in the distance. Best it should glug under and sink to the depths, never to be discovered or raised.

I peer out across the valley to a point where smoke is pluming from a farmhouse chimney. Somewhere, tiny people are down there, and me and my brother are with them. We are strapping 1/24 scale siblings with tanned sinewy arms parking matching tractors in a dark barn. Or out of sight, behind those trees over there, we are two frozen-in-time small boys in Wellington boots, forever throwing stones across a stream. A woman with realistic looking tied back hair, wearing round sunglasses with yellow lenses, is calling from the kitchen window that lunch is served.

Doors bang. Boots are kicked off in hallways. Taps run in bathrooms, and still-grubby hands are wiped on freshly washed white towels. In the kitchen, the table is already set, and salad, sprouted shoots and fucking rice cakes are not the centrepiece. No. There's more than that. Much more.

Thick vegetable soup. Hunks of crusty white bread and a full block of butter. Chicken legs. Slices of ham. Dips. Chips. Coleslaw. A selection of cheeses — Edam, Cheddar, Brie, Roquefort. Steaming fruit pies. Chocolate cake. Scones. A pot of clotted cream. Jam.

We are ravenous.

Chair legs scrape on slate floors. Red wine glugs from a carafe into heavy green tumblers. Apple juice is poured into brightly coloured plastic beakers.

And then we eat.

Long Time, No See
Biro and marker pen on paper 150 x 190cm

We do hope that you have enjoyed reading this large print book.

Did you know that all of our titles are available for purchase?

We publish a wide range of high quality large print books including:
Romances, Mysteries, Classics
General Fiction
Non Fiction and Westerns

Special interest titles available in large print are:
The Little Oxford Dictionary
Music Book
Song Book
Hymn Book
Service Book

Also available from us courtesy of Oxford University Press:
Young Readers' Dictionary
(large print edition)
Young Readers' Thesaurus
(large print edition)

For further information or a free brochure, please contact us at:
Ulverscroft Large Print Books Ltd.,
The Green, Bradgate Road, Anstey,
Leicester, LE7 7FU, England.
Tel: (00 44) 0116 236 4325
Fax: (00 44) 0116 234 0205

Other titles published by Ulverscroft:

2 A.M. AT THE CAT'S PAJAMAS

Marie-Helene Bertino

Madeleine is two days away from being ten. She needs a haircut, is unofficially forbidden from singing in church or school assembly, and smokes Newport Menthols from the carton her mother was smoking when she died at the beginning of the year. Her mother had filled a recipe box with instructions on how to do various things she knew she wouldn't be around to teach her daughter: how to make a fist; how to change a flat tire; how to write a thank-you note for a gift you hate. And one card, she listed the rules of singing. The #1 rule: KNOW YOURSELF . . .

THE WATER IS WIDE

Liz Gilbey

Artist Mikki Webster takes her beloved narrow-boat, *Serendipity*, on a holiday tour of Britain's waterways, stopping in at Bleakhall to visit her brother Jonny and his wife Tracy. The couple have their hands full — renovating their canal-side cottage, launching their new careers, and coping with an imminent baby as well as their rebellious teenager Katie. When Katie has a serious motorbike accident, Mikki stays moored beside Wharf Cottage in order to lend a hand. But sparks fly when Mikki, working at the boatyard, encounters Bill Rankin — the pop star she had fallen in love with all those years ago . . .

BEYOND REASON

Gwen Kirkwood

Young Janet Scott loves books and learning, and is happy living at the schoolhouse wher her grandfather is the dominie. Her world is shattered when he dies and the new schoolmaster's petty cruelty becomes intolerable. Sent to work for farmer Wull Foster, Janet becomes the target of his dangerous lechery, and escapes. Taken in by the kind philanthropist Josiah Saunders, an old friend of her grandfather's, she is pitched into a dilemma when he offers her the security of an amiable but passionless marriage. For her heart belongs to another: her childhood friend, the penniless lawyer's clerk Fingal McLauchlan . . .

APHRODITE'S ISLAND

Hilary Green

1955: The island of Cyprus is torn apart by EOKA's insurrection against British rule. Seventeen-year-old Ariadne's family are deeply involved in the rebellion, guarding hidden caches of rifles to arm the militants. But when British soldier Stephen Allenby arrives to search their house, a spark ignites between him and Ariadne: despite their divided loyalties, the two fall in love . . .
1973: Back in England, Stephen labours under the twin shadows of a strained marriage and miserable job. Then the rise of EOKA-B sends him back to Cyprus as a foreign correspondent and information-gatherer, all the while searching the island for the memories of his youth . . .

THE LIVING

Léan Cullinan

The Troubles may be officially over but, for the first generation to come of age in Ireland's flimsy peacetime, the ghosts of the past are all too close to home . . . Cate Houlihan is adrift in a life that doesn't feel her own, struggling with a new job at an eccentric publishing house and stifled by overbearing parents. When romance blossoms with the gorgeous, intelligent — and British — Matthew Taylor, it seems as if things might finally be going her way. But Cate's job brings her into contact with the country's Republican past. And the lines between this, her family, and her new relationship are beginning to blur . . .